INTENTIONAL DISSONANCE

a book about falling

iain s. thomas

central
avenue
publishing

2012

This Central Avenue Publishing edition is published by arrangement with
Iain S. Thomas.

www.centralavenuepublishing.com

First print edition published by Central Avenue Publishing,
an imprint of Central Avenue Marketing Ltd.

INTENTIONAL DISSONANCE

ISBN 978-1-926760-86-5 (pbk)
ISBN 978-1-926760-85-8 (ebk)

Published in Canada
Printed in United States of America

1. FICTION/Dystopian   2. FICTION/Science Fiction

Cover Design: Lloyd Foggit

Follow the author on twitter @iwrotethisforu

For my father and mother,
for teaching me to do what I love and for making me, me.

INTENTIONAL DISSONANCE

THE END

You have read this all before and you will again. Do you think you're in the bookshop now, just browsing? Are you in front of your computer, previewing the first few pages? Or is this a well-thumbed tattered old thing that lives next to your bed? Or is it sleeping, lost and forgotten at the back of a bookshelf?

No matter. You have read this all before and you will again.

Have you ever stopped and wondered if, really, you're just living the same few seconds over and over again and you just don't know it? You'd never know. Maybe you've been doing the same thing for one thousand years. Sometimes that happens. Like when you're reading and you get a thought stuck in your head and you find your eyes just glazing over the words and you have to go back and read the same thing again.

No matter. You have read this all before and you will again.

You have read this before.

This is what happens, when I fall.

CHAPTER 1

NOW

Something incredibly sad.

What follows is what happens each time I fall. I do not know if these things really happen but this is what I believe happens. As your eyes move across these words, some sacred engine is coming back to life and I am beginning to fall again. Sometimes, it feels like floating.

If you do not mind, I will refer to myself as Jon, in the third person, as these things happen.

I understand that talking about Jon as "I" instead of "Jon" would perhaps make more sense, as I am the one telling you what's happening, not some omniscient voice somewhere up in the clouds. But one of my earliest memories is of my father, narrating the things I did as I ran around the house or played outside. Like a commentator for a football match, he would yell, "Jon goes up the swing and down the swing, look at him go! He's a champion!" or "Jon's eating his spaghetti like a master, ladies and gentlemen, let's see if he can finish in time or if we'll have another disaster like we did with the vegetables the other night!"

So talking about himself in the third person in his mind, where no one but you gets to go, gives Jon (still me) a certain degree of confidence. Or maybe it's just that old habits die hard. Anyway, this is now and in this now, this is what's happening to the remaining humans in the last city on Earth.

"A space station has recovered Eliot Philips, an astronaut who was spun out into space in a refueling accident and now, his body has returned after completing an orbit around the earth which has lasted more than thirty years."

The screen on the side of the giant black floating news zeppelin shows a picture of an old woman, presumably Philips' widow, identifying a young frozen corpse as she weeps tears she has been holding on to for far too long. The zeppelin hovers like a bumblebee over the city. Below the floating news screen, the white marble spires of the United Government building, the last great monument man has built, reach for the heavens, each one raised as if in a challenge to some unseen and unknown adversary. Jon turns to look at them, breaking the audio feed into his head from the news zeppelin and the sudden silence brings to an end his wandering day dream. He can make out the building's spires all the way on the other side of NewLand, past the mostly empty and unused ornate buildings, lecture rooms, theaters and gymnasiums that blossom strictly from each side of the intricate streets, even through the grimy windows of Emily's hodgepodge, trinket-filled apartment. Low-hanging old lights cast a strange glow over the room and are complemented by the flickering lights from one of the first teleporters ever made. The teleporter hums for a second, like it might spring back to life, but it doesn't. It's broken forever. The government has asked that Emily collect and keep old things, should the world ever need them again. Marble statues from Greece, stone slabs containing fossils from Africa and a rainbow coloured VW Beetle from the American 60's all live uneasily together. The government likes giving people responsibilities. Jon thinks that they believe it gives people a sense of purpose.

NewLand feels like an old attic, spilling over with old secrets. Like someone has taken the leftovers of the world and dumped them in one place. This place. The last living place. Through the window, Jon regards one impossibly perverse spire which has bits of the Eiffel Tower sticking out of it. It was rudely salvaged, and carelessly erected. Industrial teleporters—when they were still allowed—brought it here

3

along with the Acropolis, the Statue of Liberty, and several other things that were considered "worth keeping." It acts as a reminder of what the human race was once capable. Now there are less than a few million people left on the planet. Black smoke rises out of stacks from the dark machines rumbling below the building, the only noise to be heard as figures move silently from building to building. The grey buildings are all closely piled together like set pieces in a play, short balconies hanging over doors, just a few steps from their neighbour across the road. Some people have painted their doors bright, festive colours but most are a simple, uniform grey. It is a terminally depressed world and yet the people drift past, each individual wearing an immovable grin. No, that's wrong. Some grinned. Some smiled. Some raised their eyebrows and smiled with their eyes, and no one said much. What's left to talk about? How happy you are? People live, die, and smile as they do each.

It's been nearly ten years since the world ended. Or it may as well have. Jon's a man in the twilight of his twenties now and his delicate frame holds his clothes as best it can.

Outside, across the road from him, a little blonde girl in a pink dress runs down the pavement outside into her father's sweat-soaked arms. The father shoots wildly with a stolen pistol at the police teleporting in, who are yelling at him to stop. As she grips his neck with her tiny arms and holds tight, a single shot fired from a young sergeant hits the father in the shoulder, sending a spray of blood into the air, just missing his daughter's head. His blue eyes go red and his face grimaces in pain, but still he instinctively whips his body in front of her, his only daughter, and they fall backwards into the bright blue light behind them; a light coming from the stolen government teleporter the man, apparently, has illegally modified. And then silence for a second. Then a little blonde girl in a pink dress suddenly appears outside and runs down the pavement outside into her father's arms, who's shot in the shoulder, again. They have looped like this, for years. They're just ghosts. The theory is that the man's illegal modifications caused this infinite loop but no one really seems to know what causes the teleporters to loop, just that they do. And now humankind must deal with chronological waste sites, where teleporters have terminally jammed. It must watch the same thing, again and again.

There are thousands of these waste sites and these ghosts are the reason that access to technology has been extremely limited. Jon stops watching. He's been absent-mindedly playing with his father's brass pocket watch, turning it over and over in his hands, feeling the engraving with his fingers: *You will become whatever you want to become.* He returns it to his inside jacket pocket, where it's close to his heart. The view of this particular ghost, this endless loop of a quite famous bank robber trying to rescue or kidnap his daughter—depending on who you speak to or what newspaper you read; there are only two newspapers that are still published for the remaining populace, and they still disagree with each other—once drove the property prices sky-high amongst the last humans.

But now, this place, like the little girl outside, is just another ghost.

If teleportation were still allowed, at least the food from the one remaining commercial airline wouldn't be wasted. It could simply be teleported off the plane, onto the table of any starving person. There were once plenty of starving people, all over the world. But not now. Back then, everyone wanted to work in New York, have lunch in Paris and pay rent in rural India. But no one figured on the ghosts. People got caught in endless loops when the machines malfunctioned or were modified or were used on Sundays. The excuses were numerous but it soon became clear that the technology just wasn't stable. At first, the looping ghosts were shrouded with tarpaulins, wherever and however it was happening, surrounded by police tape but people seemed to care less and less and many found some kind of fascination in watching moments and people repeat themselves endlessly. The people in them never know. For them, it is always now.

Jon is full of these things, feelings and thoughts, not just in his heart but in his head. The first thing taken out in the war that followed The End, the common name for the day it all went to shit, the great reckoning of mankind, was the Statue of Liberty. If you squint you can see the remaining bits: a spike from her crown, an eyebrow, a hand with a torch. Apparently, you can still see the book she once held, if you get close enough. Bombers dropped a billion tons of hate and fire on it. Jon should know, he used to fly one of those bombers. They were told that they were destroying an enemy but he can't remember the details. No one was allowed to remember the details. Now, even without the memories and with so few things left, the war was clearly about resources. The remains of the earth. Mankind has been reduced to a scavenging dog and its ribs are showing. Besides the algae farms far outside of NewLand, there's barely a patch of land left on the planet that can grow even the stubbornest weed.

He turns his head and looks past the remains of the Eiffel Tower, to get a better look at Lady Liberty's crown of thorns. This is another thing he keeps inside himself, this piece of knowledge about the bombings, the things that cause ruins and remains and survivors. It is a thing that makes him clench his jaw. He knows they take the families of "enemy" aviators and strap them, alive, to the sides of their aircraft in glass coffins. Military airfields are often filled with screams before takeoff, as young girls and boys, wives, mothers and fathers are lead towards the aircraft to be strapped in. And so all pilots know that when they shoot at the enemy, there's a chance that they're killing their own, or a friend's family.

And while the pilots weep as they fight, neither side's generals allow themselves to care. This is/was/could be war, after all. Thousands lived. More died. There doesn't seem to be much enemy left. Or anyone really.

Jon carries on looking out the dirty window and stretches his long fingers out and back in again and again like he's squeezing an invisible ball. His fingers miss playing with the pocket watch but that habit irritates him. Faint memories of what once happened crash through his mind. Different memories do the same in the street, through the weak, tenuous fabric of now, riddled with holes from billions of people jumping back and forth from place to place, shadows and glimmers, caught in loops forever.

Jon tells his head to shut up and he picks up a tiny rust-red vial off the Venetian-carved antique table. He examines the lime-green writing on it before holding it above his mouth. He can't read the word properly but he thinks it starts with an "S." Exactly three drops land on his tongue and he counts them off carefully as they fall.

Lacrymatory: Lat. lacrima - a tear. A bottle used to collect the tears of mourners at funerals, found in ancient Roman and Greek tombs, normally made of glass but occasionally also terra cotta.

The drops taste like peach iced tea. It is sweet, not harsh at all.

"What's this one called?" asks Jon, swallowing, turning the vial over and over in his hands.

"Saudade," says Emily. "It's a Portuguese word for the almost terminal, endless longing for a lost love."

"Cute."

She can hear him because she's spent a good portion of her life practicing hearing him, no matter how quietly he speaks. Her red hair follows her shoulders down her back and her eyes are deep blue, deeper than Jon's, speckled with flint and green. Jon does not think about the curves behind her Victorian blue dress. They are friends and always have been, nothing more. Jon, instead, thinks that Saudade, the drug he's just put on his tongue which causes one to be overwhelmed by emotion, is a bit like Limerence (again, another word used to describe an endless longing for love) or Stendhal Syndrome (the term used to describe being bought to tears by a work of art), which is what he'd had the first time he'd tried Sadness with her. But this has slightly more of a body rush because he can feel the tips of his fingers start to tingle and go numb. He walks around Emily's dirty, cluttered little apartment, which is filled with antiques and the bric-a-brac of mankind, while his legs can still hold him, hands still opening and closing, breathing like they're lungs. His eyes glance out the window, sick of the bank robber and his daughter with the blonde hair and the pink dress looping outside, hoping in vain for something more moving to look at. *Please, God, give me something else to look at than an old fire escape and this hopeful, desperate father.* Still, the fire escape with its rust and its textures has its own kind of nobility, a defiance of some kind, because it still stands, which is so much more than can be said of so many things these days.

In the distance, he thinks he sees someone falling from the top spire of the United Government building. But it might just be crows and shadows.

He runs his fingers through his shortly cropped, dyed silver-white hair. He can feel Emily watching him. She does that sometimes, just out the corner of her eye. Jon is glad she let him in. She'd already closed up for the day when he came tapping on her door. After some hesitation and a lot of cajoling and threatening and then whispering on his part, she'd let him in and he'd hugged her and he'd felt the relief flood through him as he stepped inside, as all junkies do when they see their dealer. The rust and the decay on the fire escape reminded him of when he'd worked on one of the army airfields years after The End. He remembers his friend James, Gentle James some had called him because he found a rat and took care of it, making it his pet. He'd have done the same with any animal. Anyway, James or Gentle James or Private James Stapleton or whatever you want to call him, died midflight during an operation they'd both gone on. Something secret. The memories of everyone on board had been erased afterwards, as always, but Jon remembers the burial; they'd let him keep that. Some might have called it beautiful but it's hard to call a funeral beautiful. Because James died in flight (Jon couldn't remember how), the crew did a traditional burial at air, covering him in a kind of liquid magnesium. Then Jon, Jon and the other members of the crew that weren't needed to fly the giant bomber, threw him out of the plane with a giant crucifix chained to him, and Jon remembers so vividly, as the body of the person who used to be his friend, sweet Gentle James, kissed the air, the magnesium burst into white hot flames. He became an angel of bright light and smoke and then nothing. Ashes in the sky. Ashes in the sky. Now Jon's trying not to think about it but there was a fire escape just like the one outside on a building in that fucking airfield. Every day, he walked through the buildings and when no one was looking, he took out a spanner and stole bolts out of things, from the computers, from the walkways, from the machines, whatever. One at a time. Nothing anyone would notice. But the place was always falling apart and no one could work out why. He once had bottles and bottles of nuts and bolts stored away. They would've killed him if they'd found them. He didn't know why he did it; sometimes people just do things. Maybe he just hated his job and the people he worked for.

After he'd finished his years of service, he decided that since there weren't any normal jobs left, he wanted to be a conceptual art dealer. Someone who just sells the idea of art to other people. You'd pay him some money and he'd whisper poetry or special secrets in your ear; like, "My art, which fathered heaven." But apparently that job didn't really exist for a reason: whispering poetry is not a sustainable way to make a living. Perhaps in a good, benevolent world, poets would be rich and stock brokers would go home to shacks, but there weren't any more stockbrokers and there were almost as many poets left. So a magician it was. An illusionist. A conjurer.

He didn't know any magic tricks though, so he cheated.

He didn't even need the top hat or the white ruffled shirt. Before that, when he was still considering the conceptual art dealer thing, he'd once tried to sell the idea of brushing your hair at the same time as everyone else who bought the idea from him, so that whenever you brushed your hair, you'd know that you weren't alone and that somewhere out there, someone else was brushing their hair, too. He thought it'd be beautiful, that because, despite all the anti-depressants these days, people still needed cheering up, people needed company, even if it was a strange kind of company. Even if it was just the knowledge that somewhere else, someone else was feeling the exact same thing as you at the exact same time as you. But no one had wanted to give him money for it, everyone just looked at him strangely and that's why everyone still brushes their hair at different times. Stupid world. Stupid, dying world.

He'd gotten a job for a while as a paparazzi for hire. People would ask him to take pictures of them in the company of potential lovers, to create the idea that the person those potential lovers were talking to was a big deal, such a big deal that a photographer wanted to follow him or her around and take pictures of them. It didn't last long. Jon was too quiet. He didn't yell enough, according to most of his previous clients and when he did yell, it was sometimes rude.

Now, back here in this apartment, Emily puts three drops on her own tongue and smiles before slipping her shoes off and taking a few paces over the rich Persian carpet Jon's standing on, standing a little nearer to him.

Emily undoes the band in her hair and her red hair falls.

"Do you want music? I can put on some Ambient Music For Airports maybe? Or some of Maynard James Keenan's last works if you'd like?" asks Emily.

"No, the sound of you yammering on is music enough to my ears."

"You're a bit of a bastard, Jon. You know that right?" Emily smiles.

Jon just nods, lost somewhere in things that have already happened and smiles back at Emily, despite all the random things bumping around in his head.

She shrugs and makes her own choices for the music they'll need. Even though she knows he almost never answers or if he does, it's with sarcasm, she feels it'd be impolite to stop asking.

Brian Eno's opening notes of 1/1 fill the room, washing everything with an almost-tangible pink haze. The vinyl worked. The technology ration Emily had spent getting it was worth it and it returned that soft texture modern technology had once missed. Digital bits have no colour and less texture. But this piano, this piano being played in this song keeps the sound and colour coming at him, breaking over him like a wave, before it reaches Jon's throat. The drug, the Sadness, is working, breaking the horrible, dull, boring, mind-numbing happiness imposed on him and everyone else in NewLand by the antidepressants in the city's water supply. Jon almost never drank water and if he did, it was an emergency and he was dying. He hated that feeling when he had to, the numbness, the death smile, the lying of the soul. Nothing felt real. The world felt at bay. So he drank crudely bottled water, collected from the rain that still fell and then was filtered. It was either that or beer. Some of the Sadness junkies lived on beer but that seemed like a hollow existence. Hundreds of years ago, it was almost always safer to drink clean beer than dirty water. Now, history has repeated itself; you either drank the water or dealt with the overwhelming depression that had existed since the day of The End. It was so bad if you were out on a hot day and didn't have enough water to drink, some were just as likely to die from suicide as heat stroke.

"Can you feel it?" asks Emily. A single, hot tear runs down her cheek, ruining her make up.

Jon remembers a word.

Frisson: The word used to describe the moment the hair on the back of your neck stands up when you are struck by a climax of beauty in art.

"Yes," whispers Jon. "Fuck, yes…" He bursts into hot, shuddering sobs. "…yes."

Jon's feelings completely overwhelm him, rolling over him like an unstoppable black wave. The light inside goes dark. This is a kind of chemically induced sadness but it's so fucking beautiful. He digs his fingernails into his palm, trying desperately to create some kind of physical manifestation of what he's feeling, trying to bring it out and make it all real. To make him real again, to feel something one more time.

The world quickens and he falls backwards in his mind and here, out of it. If Jon is capable of real, objective thought at this point, it might strike him that beyond the obvious, there's little to be sad about in this moment. No acid rain fell on his way home to Michelle, the girl, then woman, he has loved without question for ten long years. No songs reminded him of his father dying on the day the world ended or his mother who lasted only a little bit longer. No phone not ringing. No reminder of his past or present or future.

And so Jon descends into warmer places, a rich and fertile crystal garden of feeling and emotion. Really though, he's on the dusty carpet, slowly surrounded by light. It's soft, white, and you can almost touch it.

A voice from nowhere, from the air itself, whispers, "It's all going to be ok."

It reminds him of the last time he saw his father: his father held him, then gave him a pill and Jon fell asleep in his arms. Then, in his mind, he sees the image of a fascist bastard Peace Ambassador, one of those entrusted to uphold the peace in NewLand, holding the limp body of a child that had been hit by a passing carriage, and the cop, he's crying, the soulless scum is crying. Jon saw that walking home once. Each feeling hits Jon full force in the chest and then appears in front of his mind's eye, represented by different vivid visions, the black wave washing over him, again and again like a relentless tide.

It feels like he's falling forever. He clutches his knees, turning himself into a ball. The world is brought into terrible, beautiful focus. Everything is tragic and wonderful at the same time.

Nerves flare, synapses snap and shivers run up and down his body, like someone's running their hand over him, just a hair's breadth above his skin but never actually touching.

He remembers the first time he'd felt pain and had a name for it; stepping on a green piece of glass, a broken bottle in the gravel driveway of his parents' small, white suburban house. He remembers being in a row boat once with his father and mother and noticing the way swans move without moving and it's so beautiful, it's all so beautiful. Abstract phenomena, memories, stories, symbols, and metaphors crash through his mind, one after the other.

He opens his eyes and manages to blink away some of the hot tears. Emily has fallen on her back, on some pillows, on the Persian rug, on the parquet floor; the same thing consuming him is consuming her, eating her whole, burning her up. She moves at a thousand frames a second, her eyes open and a steady stream of tears falls down past her ear, into her falling hair. Her make-up leaves dark trails across her face.

Everything falls.

She falls.

He falls with her.

She's slowly beautiful and even in all its current sadness, even in so much chaos, so is the world. Even though it's all fucked up. Even now. It's years since it all happened and so much has changed.

Her chest falls as his rises.

CHAPTER 2

THEN

A plane flies overhead and inside it is a writer who has
spent most of his life as a law clerk, even though he's
always known deep down that he's a writer. For the first
time, he's worked out what he wants to write, what the
truth really is. He begs a napkin and a pen off the air
hostess and he writes down the most beautiful sentence
ever written, as the engine catches fire outside and the
plane starts its plummet to the ground. It doesn't matter
to him. It's the only sentence he's ever written and it is the
last and no part of him cares. The sentence falls through
the air with singed, black edges and comes to rest in a
tree, in a park, miles away. One day, around ten years
from now, an old widow of an astronaut will find it when a
strong breeze finally blows it from its hiding place. She will
read it and she will weep.

The kitchen is covered in plants and Jon's father patiently trims a
bonsai. Jon's friend James once said that his father had green fingers
and that made Jon spend a lot of time when he was younger trying to
imagine what that meant. Outside, the oak tree where Jon's old swing
still hung breathed slowly back into the world, leaning backwards and
forwards into the early evening air. The oak tree had been Jon's best
friend when he was younger. He was always climbing, turning its fallen
branches into swords and spending time beneath its shade, reading.

Jon's father has tried to get him to learn maths. He's tried so hard.

Jon sometimes thinks he's adopted, just every now and again, because surely if his father is good at maths, shouldn't he be good at maths, too? Isn't that how genetics worked? Don't you get the same abilities, the same talents that your parents have? Apparently not. Jon's father, Peter Salt, is working on the cutting edge of human technology: teleportation, genetic transformation, white/black hole looping, things that shouldn't be invented but are in the process of happening, in the process of becoming real, everyday things. There's a lot of work meetings that leave his father with his head in his hands and when anyone asks what's wrong, he always tells them the same thing: he's not allowed to say. Jon is not going to get the same job as his father. He knows that. Jon likes to pretend he doesn't care that he's ridiculously bad at all these things but it gets to him and he does actually care. His father patiently sits with him at the old wooden table in the living room, repeating the numbers over and over again, repeating the ways and mechanics that made the numbers turn into other numbers, hoping they somehow, in some way, start to make sense. The words make sense to Jon, their letters hover in the air to make beautiful patterns, like "S-e-7-e-n" but the numbers never do. The numbers are just words. He doesn't understand. He'd once tried to replace parts of the words with numb3r5 8ut th4t d1dn't accomplish anything beyond making him more confused and really, really upsetting his maths teacher.

It makes him feel alien. Sometimes, he aches and gets angry and that core of ache and anger builds on itself again and again until he's a walking ball of ache. Maybe other children see this in him because they can see these things easier and aren't afraid to say something about it. Or at least, haven't been taught yet to ignore it and move past it.

Right now, Jon has a distant look on his face. The kind you can read from a few steps away. Something about his posture or the way he moves things around the table or the way he doesn't really answer questions. A machine that could be a microwave *bings* and Jon's father leaves the bonsai, walks over to the microwave and takes out a steaming bowl.

"Try this," says Jon's dad and he gives him a bowl of what looks like melted, grey cheese. He has a crop of grey-dusted blonde hair. Jon stabs some with his fork, puts it in his mouth and immediately spits it out.

"It tastes like rotting fish," says Jon, still spitting.

"Whoops. It's supposed to taste like fresh fish."

"What is it?"

"We're trying to recreate food using different kinds of algae. With the right combination, in the future, we might be able to recreate any kind of taste and any kind of texture."

"That's exciting," says Jon but he doesn't mean it.

"What's wrong with you?"

"Nothing."

"You can't bullshit a bullshitter and your old man's a bullshitter, Jon. What's wrong?"

"I got kicked out of the band," says Jon under his breath.

"Why?"

Jon doesn't immediately respond.

"They said I suck as a guitarist," says Jon. "But they're the ones that suck."

"Do you?"

"Do I what?"

"Do you suck?"

"A real dad wouldn't ask that question."

"You don't have a real dad, there's just me, the unreal dad."

"Maybe."

"Maybe what?"

"Jesus, maybe I suck as a guitarist, ok? Are you trying to make me emo?"

"I don't know what that last word you used means and something tells me I don't really care to know."

"That's because you hate me."

"Yeah, that's why I bought you that guitar in the first place, because I hate you so much. How many times this week have you practiced?" asks Jon's dad.

Jon shrugs and turns away from his father.

"Jon, pay attention for once: people become the things they want to. If you really wanted to be a guitar player, you'd start by just wanting to play the guitar. And if you want to play the guitar, you'll play every day because that's what you enjoy. That's what you'd want to do. Are you sure you don't just want to be famous? Do you want to be a rock star?"

"I don't know," says Jon, "Maybe. So what?"

"Well, then that's not wanting to play the guitar. People become what they want to become. Dancers, dance. Writers, write. Famous guitarists are famous because they're very good at playing guitar and they're very good because they play every day and they play every day because they love to play the guitar. People who just want to be famous, just spend their lives wanting to become famous. Or actors maybe. You won't become anything you don't actually want to become," says Jon's dad and he puts his hand on his son's shoulder.

Jon nods slowly.

"I'm not trying to make you feel better. We hate each other remember? You're going to be a man soon and I want you to understand how life works. If you want a hug and the words, 'It's all going to be ok,' go and watch a movie. Life isn't a movie. Life is real," says Jon's dad and Jon gives him a hug because he loves him.

Jon turns around slowly and starts walking out the room, now lost in his head, trying to work out if he just wants to be famous or learn to play the guitar.

"Go to sleep," calls Jon's dad after him and despite everything, you know that he loves his son, so much.

Later, Jon is lying in his bed, trying to sleep. The walls are filled with posters of superheroes and he thinks it'd be easier to be one of them right now. His favourite poster, from *The Black Kracken*, takes pride of place in the centre of the wall. His dad had once asked him what made it so special and Jon had tried to explain about the mystical pirate ship, about the crew of one-eyed space pirates that floated through space on it protecting each other and the universe from behind their black cloth masks. They never spoke. They only communicated with each other and the outside world by writing. Something about them made them special to Jon and it was the one comic that his father had ever bothered discussing with him. The rest were just filled with monsters. Monsters. You can fight a monster. You can't fight maths.

He has a HUGE maths test tomorrow that he didn't even tell his father about and now, there's nothing he can do about studying for it. Going to bed early makes more sense to him than staying up and studying. He finds studying hard. It's hard to think about the same thing for too long. His brain flitters back and forth over things like a desperate moth. He spends a lot of time inside his head; it's a beautiful place. He's never had a fear of missing out, just a fear of joining in. This makes him bad at some things and good at other things. He's staring at the ceiling and the light from the hallway coming in the gap between the door and the frame is like a lance made of pure light, keeping the darkness at bay. That's what he told himself when he was really small; it's a lance made of liquid fire and if anything truly bad, truly monstrous ever comes in here or appears out of the ground or breaks through the ceiling or however monsters enter a room, he'll just reach out and somehow that lance of pure white light will be real and he'll take it and drive it straight through the monster and kill it with light.

Jon is getting closer to sleep now. Random thoughts are flooding through his head, words and numbers, pictures and places, and he jumps through them like an acrobat slowly arcing between giant cinema screens. Those screens are slowing down now and Jon is approaching a dream; it's probably going to be about being unprepared for school. At the edge of consciousness, he's called back by something.

Nothing.

He starts drifting back to sleep, then he hears it again. There's a noise in the dark. Someone or something is knocking softly on his bedroom window.

CHAPTER 3

NOW

Somewhere in the distance, an algae farm is wrapping up for the day and the workers are retreating to their tiny sleeping and living cubicles where most will sell their dreams to the last corporations left on Earth, looking for fresh research and innovative new ideas for exciting new product lines, which will then be sold back to the remains of the world. A woman with silvery brown hair falls asleep as soon as her head hits the pillow, her dreams no longer her own.

Meanwhile, somewhere else, Jon worries that she's felt too much and maybe now there's nothing left to feel. He worries that he might run out of things to give her to feel but he tells himself that every day, he will have enough to give and she will have something for him in return when he gives it; a smile, even a slight curve of the lip was more than enough. He discovered that night, now so long ago, after an entire childhood of feeling like something was missing, that she was all he'd ever wanted, her and that slight curve of her lip. And so Jon takes the steam train, the last real public transport available, home to Michelle.

His father used to take him on the train, a normal electric one, as a treat and this experience, the sound of the tracks, the gentle sway from side to side and the world rushing by, rhythmically, in bursts of houses and bursts of nothing, makes Jon think about him. It's something he instantly regrets as he makes eye contact with someone else, an old man, maybe homeless, on the other side of the steam train. He always worries that people can feel what he's feeling if he makes eye contact with them while he's feeling it.

How could something that affected you so intensely be a private experience? Surely the people around you could pick up on the soft water in your eyes, the moment of strain passing like a shadow across your face.

He'd decided long ago he didn't want anyone else inside him but him. Especially not anyone from this leftover hell. He'd heard someone say that there were pigeons at the zoo. He'd like to take Michelle and go and see them. No one has seen one in years. It's just the crows now; the only real bird population to speak of. And the crows are everywhere, circling like black clouds before a storm. The train passes ruin after ruin of what were once suburbs and shops, now burnt-out empty shells, covered with graffiti and with broken windows that made the buildings look like they were weeping for what once was. An overpass has the words: 'Beware: Here be shadows.' like an epitaph scrawled across it in blood-red paint. It tells him that he's approaching his station.

He gets off at the station and walks the few hundred feet to their apartment, swipes his arm in front of the sensor at the main door, steps over the sleeping street kids and climbs the five flights of stairs to their apartment. He unlocks the door as quietly as he can; she's sleeping. He gets into bed with Michelle. It's just a mattress on a floor but it's their mattress on the floor. Everything's a mess here. It contrasts starkly with the clichéd chrome and glass design of the apartment. White walls and sharp corners. If you burnt everything in the room except the carpet and the walls, you could've shot the interior for some glossy, old-fashioned design magazine and people would think to themselves: "One day, I want to own nothing and live there, in that clean white space."

His clothes are strewn across the floor. Some have just been to the laundry and some haven't and he really doesn't care. There are one or two plates lying around, and numerous bills and forms and other previously useless pieces of paper now have Lacrymatory vials lying on them, serving the perverse purpose of helping Jon keep track of which vials still have something in them. Michelle never seems to care. He loves her as much as he did the night he first met her at the park. She has crystal-blue eyes and he remembers being told that everyone with blue eyes was once infected by a plague and that disturbance in their genetics gave them blue eyes. He wonders if everyone with blue eyes has a common sense of loss, somewhere in the back of their soul, not ever quite knowing what it is but knowing that they once suffered and now would always be marked for it. Jon places his hand softly on her back, just trying to touch the soft, almost invisible hair, not her skin. She reminds him of every good day he's ever had. Every summer spent in fields of grass. Every sunrise. Every sunset. She tastes like dew and smells like light. And when she speaks, it's like someone slowly plucking the strings of a guitar, a sadly beautiful song starting to play, all his own. And he loves her. He loves her like he can never grab enough of her between his fingers. And no matter how close he gets, even when they make love, it never feels close enough, like her flesh and her bones keep something sacred in them, hidden from him.

She is a constant comfort in the mess that is their apartment. Jon cares more about how he feels, how comfortable he is, than what things look like where he lives. Some people can't function in a mess. He can. He remembered someone asking him once how he found anything. It was easy. Whatever it was, it was somewhere on the floor.

He does his best to slow down his mind and eventually, he falls asleep next to her. After dreaming feverishly, a side effect of all the Sadness, he wakes up again. He vaguely remembers being taken to a camp where they cut the tattoos off people so they have no reminders of who they once were. Nothing left but scars. But he isn't sure that ever happened. His mind is a timeless wasteland with moments of sanity, burnt by the fire of his reservations about the rest of world and what it's become. Anyone besides him and Michelle and Emily, everyone else, could go to hell. The world could go deeper into hell. Here, at least, there was peace. They'd only spent a week in the apartment but from the looks of things, it seems longer.

They'd been thrown out of the previous one. It started out well but because of the combination of Jon's gift and the drugs, the sadness settled in; slowly, like morning fog, it seeped out through the front door into the hallway. He'd smiled when the landlord came over to ask if he knew anything about the sadness, grinned in fact, and insisted that while he didn't mind the questions, the idea that he should be anything but euphoric was ridiculous. But they always catch you sooner or later, all it takes is a tear in a mirror or a sigh as you pass. The neighbours always noticed. Most didn't say anything, quietly enjoying the idea of feeling something for the first time in years, but someone always spoke up. And then Jon and Michelle got thrown out.

He dreamed of a world where now wasn't a place in his head, where the past ate up the future one moment at a time like it should, but as his music teacher once said before she'd died in The End, "You take too many flights of fancy. You're a daydream away from the edge."

Now. Now. Now. Now.

Jon manages to fall asleep again for a few hours and when he wakes up, he kisses Michelle on the cheek. She rolls over in her sleep, not even acknowledging he's there. He leaves her in bed. He's recorded a dozen meals on the MicroPVR over the last 24 hours and he opens and closes the black plastic door, tasting each one to see if he actually wants to eat it or if he's just curious. He loves classic American dishes like pizza and hamburgers and has scheduled the box to record each and every one of those meals when they get transmitted. He tries not to think about his father. He has to perform his "magic" tonight and the knowledge sits at the back of his head, uncomfortably taking up space. The food becomes little more than a distraction. He can only do what he does, use his gift, if he's completely convinced he can do it or if he's in a state of primal fear. But the craftsmanship, the details that make it beautiful, that happens late at night when he's supposed to sleep, when he worries that maybe, this time, he will fail.

The fear drives him.

A few hours later, he's on a train and not sure how he got there. No matter, the blackouts happen often enough that he's used to them. He gets off at the station and walks the rest of the way, carrying his black suitcase, which, if asked, he tells people is filled with props for his magic tricks. The black suitcase often just contains exotic sandwiches he's downloaded off the MicroPVR. He does his best to ignore the dark shadows that make up the rest of the world. The others. The dark, depressing, damningly smiling remains of humanity, victims of drug-induced happiness and emotional manipulation, with their desperate attempts at a 'normal existence' and their disease of apartness. No matter where you go, someone's always giggling insanely in a corner somewhere, someone's stopped walking and just sat down in the middle of the road, deep in a dissociative state, a side effect of the ketamine (or at least that's the theory in terms of what they're actually using) infused water supply. A man leans out of a window, grabbing his shoulder, trying to sell him a fake pair of Fujisio TruSights™. Jon keeps walking.

Some days, he feels like they deserve the new world. The air shimmers with electricity and the butterflies in his stomach dance as he arrives under a low-hanging sign, illuminated by a few candles that crudely spell out the words, "Cabaret du Néant." He knows it's a front for Duer, a local drug dealer that supplies Sadness to Emily and pretty much the whole of the city that chooses to take it. But a job is a job, even for a "magician." Jon has never met Duer nor does he care to, based off rumours of his pastimes, which include killing or hurting people who owe him money or drugs. Jon owes him nothing and he wants to keep it that way. He opens the door. The bar is full tonight. A slight paranoia hangs over the otherwise strangely festive, jarringly-coloured, leather-clad and bowler-hatted crowd. Many wear blue bracelets that mark them as needing extra supervision for "Unnecessary Emotion." The blue bands stop them from getting jobs. After all, who wants to hire someone that isn't always happy? It shames their families and it stops them from being considered normal. Some are drinking bottled water, with none of the mood enhancing muck in it that the rest of the popu-lace gleefully consumes. Many are drinking beer. Those on the dance floor cry and scream and move and sway backwards and forwards on an unseen tide. Jon feels at least slightly at home and slightly normal here. A barman routinely squirts turpentine across the bar, across the bottles at the back, and at the supporting beams, then sets the whole thing on fire. Every time the flames whoosh out in a mini mushroom cloud, a wave of heat breaks over the crowd and they scream for more before it all burns out. Jon's seen him occasionally take out a chainsaw and rev it in time to the music. It's a nice touch.

Through a giant bay window in the side of the bar, the crowd can see a man stuck in an endless loop, chasing after his wife, who thinks he's dead and who is trying to kill herself by throwing herself off a building with a teleportation halo attached to it—a safety net that just sends you back to the top of the building when you jump. Sometimes one of the late night revelers tries to yell at her, just to see if they can stop her. Sometimes her eyes shift towards them for an instant before she falls and it happens again.

He turns away. He needs a little more of that Saudade before the show begins. He goes into the back room and past the bouncer, a burly half-man half-tree called a half-ent by society and Steve by regulars of the club. They nod at each other. Half-ents appeared shortly after The End. People began to change and with so many crazy things happening, half-human-half-trees were just one more crazy thing to add to the list. Jon often thinks that his father would have loved them, the half-ents, because he loved trees. So much that his father had worked with or dreamed of had come to pass but perhaps not in the way he would've wished. The world was a dark dream of his father. Some of the half-ents were political extremists, demanding their own separate, new rights in the new world because they were a new species. The protested. They rioted. And they did both quite violently. Fighting a tree is not as easy as it sounds. Steve, however, is not political at all. Steve, as far as Jon knows, just wants to do his job.

The back room is filled with green smoke from melancholy pipes and two children lie in the corner wearing stolen, illegally modded Tru-Sights™, their feet bare and swollen from being on the street in the cold. Their mouths hang open and they're obviously in awe of whatever they're looking at on the screens behind their glasses. Whatever place they're in is better than here.

Awe.

It's a feeling he misses. He made lists of things he wanted to feel when he was younger, big things, small things, ice, snow, the sand at the beach, someone else's hands holding his, feeling him feeling them, a feedback loop of feelings, which is what happens when two people make love. He wanted to feel things that made him feel safe and scared and things that ripped his heart out of his chest, things that made him want to go home and things that made him want to travel, things that made him proud and things that made him regret his choices and he, like all people, slowly ticked these things off the list in his head as he lived, as the world turned, until soon there were very few things left to feel.

He believed the last thing he would feel would be nothing, as that was nearly impossible to feel unless you were dead or hadn't been born yet. He wondered what it'd be like to not be able to wonder.

He'd once wanted to know what it felt like to be able to talk to people properly, to be normal but he'd given up on finding that feeling, figuring no one ever really found it.

He takes a table in the corner and puts two drops on his tongue from the small vial he's kept in his pocket since he saw Emily.

He smiles as a single tear rolls down his cheek. He's ready to go on. A man in a top hat, Barnston, the ring leader of the Cabaret, yells Jon's name into the back room. Jon's in and he's up and walking and feeling and ready and a million different things all at once. Barnston steps onto the stage, raising his top hat to the audience, and he begins to yell in a way that wouldn't be out of place at a circus: "Ladies and gentlemen of the Cabaret du Néant! Welcome to our first show of the evening. Many of you have no doubt seen magic shows before but this, this my friends is different. You will not see a woman sawn in half. You will not see a fucking rabbit pulled out of a hat. You will see things you've never seen before. You will be immersed in magic and you will witness pure, unadulterated beauty from our grandest illusionist, The Mockingbird!"

Jon hates the performing name they gave him. "The Mockingbird" just sounds stupid to him but he supposes that "Jon the Amazing" is worse. Jon steps on stage and the room hushes except for one or two people drinking and laughing in the corner. Steve, the half-ent bouncer, comes to stand in front of them and asks them to shut up without saying a word, just by folding his arms across his chest and looking at them dead on.

"A fucking magician? You want us to shut up for a magician?" says one, some strung-out freak with a head covered in braids. Steve, without missing a beat, reaches over, grabs the customer's hand and bends it back until he begs for mercy. Those who have seen him work before continue to keep those who haven't quiet. Even if they've seen Jon's abilities a thousand times, they don't want to miss a thing.

Jon starts slowly; the crowd hardly notices at first. Then a woman gasps as she looks at the wine in her hand. Tiny mermaids begin to appear in their drinks, laughing and giggling, swimming through the bubbles. A soft glow falls over everyone and everything. Jon opens his mouth and begins to sing over the melody that fills the room, the mechanics of the club's music box billowing steam, auto-tuning his words slightly while his gift turns his words into whatever everyone wants to hear, with just a hint of influence on his part. Strange sound waves drift in and out of each other.

If you weren't human, if you were a machine and incapable of seeing or hearing things as they could be, only as they are, it would sound like noise to you.

```
Spinning, shooting, shattered star,
Is it lonely where you are?
Is there a comet, in your heart?
Have you turned your absence into art?
```

The image of a woman with silver hair yet young and beautiful fills the room, like she's always been there. That's how it works. All the illusions have always just been there and you know they're there like you know you have a heart, a hand or two. It is an undeniable, simple and sudden fact.

```
Sighing, shining, splintered star,
Once so near and now so far,
Is there moonlight in your hair?
Do you close your eyes to stare?
```

"Just like rain." Emily had once said that to describe the nature of his ability. One minute it isn't and the next minute it is. And what's wrong with that? It just is. Just like the woman hovering in front of everyone with the silver hair. It seems to grow longer the more you look at it, until it becomes a grid of silver lines that form a background for the rest of her.

```
Fading, fading, faded star,
You are still my favourite scar,
Screaming out into the night
Reflecting back the darkest light
```

Her body is pale, naked and slightly translucent and somehow impossible to focus on.

```
Precious, precious, precious star
I keep your light inside a jar
Are you a stranger here on Earth?
Are you the measure of your worth?
```

Her face. There, every man sees the woman that hurt him the most, whom he'll love forever. Every woman sees herself.

```
Twinkle, twinkle, fallen star
What if love is all we are?
```

CHAPTER 4

THEN

The flag given to the son of a soldier.

He's afraid, but only a little, of the sound of knocking coming from his bedroom window. It could be a burglar or maybe some kind of assassin who knocks before they kill you; but Jon knows that his friends, the few that he has, only Emily and James really, they sometimes knock on it late at night if they want him to sneak out of the house.

Jon pulls back the curtain. Two girls are waving at him. One is Emily, who lives down the road from him. He has known her most of his life. They grew up on Blakefield Avenue together; this was their neighbourhood and once (and only once) he thought she had a crush on him. He knew he had a crush on her, also at least once. But that had passed. He doesn't know the other girl, at all. She has white-blonde hair, almost silver. They giggle as he opens the window.

"Hey, Jon," says Emily.

"Hey, Emily," says Jon.

"We were wondering if you have any cigarettes?" asks Emily.

He does. He has an entire carton that he's bought with his pocket money that month. He'd gotten an older boy to go into the supermarket to get them for him, in exchange for a box from the carton. Always worked.

"Who's we?" says Jon, eyeing the second girl up and down.

"Shut up, Jon. Do you or don't you, because we can walk to James' house too, you know."

"Sure, just give me a second," says Jon.

Jon is excited but carefully, desperately nonchalant. He can hear the second girl asking Emily if he's always like that but he ignores it; people always ask that. Of course members of the opposite sex knock on his bedroom window every night. Of course. Or so he tells himself, at least.

He scrambles back from the window to the pinewood cupboard in the corner of the room and opens the drawer at the bottom, taking out his treasure trove of things he does not want his parents to find, which includes some magazines with breasts in them, an unopened box of condoms, and the cigarettes.

"Here," he says as he hands the box of cigarettes through the window.

"Thanks, Jon," says Emily. "You're the best."

"I know."

"Whatever."

Now an awkward silence hangs between the three of them. The silver-haired one breaks it.

"Do you want to come and smoke with us?" she asks. Emily punches her in the arm.

"Ow!"

"What?"

"Don't flirt with this dork, he's my friend."

"I wasn't flirting, they're his cigarettes, surely he's allowed to come with us and smoke them."

"Whatever."

He holds the air in his lungs and then breathes out the words, "Ok, sure."

He quickly gets dressed. It isn't cold enough for shoes so he goes barefoot, in black jeans and a white t-shirt. It's still summer for a while yet and the nights are hot and humid. He starts to sneak out of the house, a time-honoured practice, stepping slowly and softly on the carpet, opening his bedroom door little by little so it doesn't squeak, the thin lance of light growing thicker until suddenly, he's bathed in the glow pouring from the bathroom across the hall. He turns a corner and the light is lost. He makes his way down the passage in the dark, feeling the walls with his hand, the frames of the doors telling him how far along the passage he is until he gets to the lounge and fiddles with the glass door, unlocking it and sliding it back. If he hadn't done it so many times, it might have made him sweat.

Finally, he's outside and they are gone, with his cigarettes.

He knew this was going to happen.

Bitches: why the hell did Emily always have to be friends with them?

He sighs and prepares himself for the trip back into the house in the dark. Then he hears giggling coming from the bushes on the front lawn. He smiles as he walks past the trees and flowers over to the big mulberry bush his mother is so proud of and he finds them hiding behind it. They burst out laughing when they see him.

It sounds so loud.

"You guys are comedic geniuses but please stop, you'll wake my parents up and they're not famous for their sense of humour," says Jon.

"Sowwy," says Emily but she doesn't seem to mean it, mainly because she crosses her eyes and says it in a stupid way.

"Grow up, Emily. Let's go to the park, it's just down the road. We can smoke there. We can't be too long," says Jon and he hopes he doesn't sound like a pussy.

Cigarettes are magical for Jon right now. He enjoys the taboo of smoking more than the actual act of smoking itself. The secret. The knowledge of doing something inherently wrong flowing through his blood, making it pump hot in his temples. The leaves crunch underfoot on the green suburban sidewalk, loudly so they step into the road. There is no one on Blakefield Avenue but them and the light from the stars; the black tar stretches away from them like an endless river. Jon does not know why but he wonders if every road is connected to every other road. Maybe if he touches it, someone, somewhere, in London, Paris, or New York will know he has touched it and they will touch it, too.

They are by the park now and they hop over the low wall separating the park from the rest of the world and they walk over to the swings, simple things made from old tires, where the three of them, Jon, Emily, and her friend sit and swing slowly back and forth. Emily slowly unwraps the clear plastic, then the gold foil, and then takes three cigarettes out and gives them one each, keeping one for herself. She looks at Jon expectantly. He reaches into his pocket and grabs empty air. He has forgotten the lighter. Jon feels a cold bucket of fear and failure pour over him. Fucking typical Jon. Way to fuck it up.

"I think I've got one," says Emily, seeing him patting his pockets furiously.

"Cool, I hoped someone else had otherwise we would've been fucked," says Jon. Just being casual. Nonchalant. That's all. He does this all the time. Sure. She takes out a cheap plastic lighter and passes it to him. Steam and smog from the industrial part of town where the coal fields and the tannery are throw a haze over the stars on the edge of the horizon and the cicadas just make noise. He lights his cigarette and inhales, the smoke filling his lungs. He does not cough. He's ever-so-slightly proud of this. He goes out every night with girls to smoke— he does this *all* the time. He keeps telling himself that. He passes the lighter back to Emily and she and her silver-haired friend light up.

And then, silence.

"Call me rude but if I'm going to be giving you cigarettes, I'd like to at least know your name," says Jon, forcing the words out. Saying things in front of the silver-haired girl feels like jumping off a cliff.

"Do you usually go to the park with girls you don't know to smoke cigarettes?"

Jon laughs and says, "All the time, you're the third lot tonight." She laughs back. Nice one, Jon.

"I'm Michelle," Michelle says.

"Hello, Michelle, I'm Jon," Jon says.

They shake hands, awkwardly. Jon isn't sure why but shaking hands does seem like the right thing to do. You can't hug someone you've just met to say hello to them. Do people do that? Jon doesn't know.

"Michelle's just moved here, she's in my class," says Emily.

"I see," says Jon. Jon strokes an imaginary beard.

The girls giggle at this and then there's another one of those moments of silence when the only sound is the swings creaking. Jon feels he is far too good at creating silence.

"What test are you writing tomorrow?" Emily asks.

"Maths," says Jon.

"Don't you mean, 'math'? Thank God you aren't writing English," says Michelle.

"Whatever," says Jon.

The girls giggle at him. He inhales smoke again and still, he does not cough. Lately, Jon is becoming conscious of the fact that he goes through phases of wanting everyone to notice him. He would try and be funny when he wanted that to happen and then he would very quickly find himself wanting everyone to forget him and he would be quiet when he wanted that to happen instead.

"Aren't you guys also writing tests?" asks Jon.

"No, we finished today, that's why we're out," says Emily.

"That's lucky," says Jon.

They are quiet again and they all start to swing slowly. The world slows for one precious, stretched-out moment and they hang in the air, legs out, leaning into gravity somewhere under the moonlight. For that one brief moment, it feels like anything is possible, that Jon can find a girl he likes, become a famous guitar player or a graphic designer (his second choice), anything, anything at all.

The possibilities are endless.

And now Jon finds Michelle strange and new and attractive and as he thinks that, he falls in love with her. Perhaps it is her laugh or her smile or something in her eyes. Whatever it is, Jon falls.

Jon decides in that very moment that he wants to spend the rest of his life with her. She has barely spoken more than a few words but there is something in the air, something about her, that makes Jon's heart beat faster when he looks at her.

It's a strange, weird love but it's true.

"So you're on holiday already?" Jon asks, his voice breaking a little. His heart makes the words fall like water from his mouth and they sound strange to him, like someone's playing him a recording of his own voice.

"Yes. Well, no, we still have to go to school tomorrow but it's not like we'll be doing anything, just filling up the time." says Michelle. She sighs and he worries that she can read minds or knows exactly what he's like inside and how nervous he suddenly is.

"I wish I had tomorrow off, instead of this test. I'd stay home and smoke cigarettes and read comic books all day," says Jon.

"You read comic books?" Michelle asks, stifling a laugh. Emily punches her arm again, and Michelle turns around and tells Emily to shush.

"Yes, I read comic books," says Jon. He likes her. Maybe she likes comic books.

"I read comic books," says Michelle, smiling at Jon through the cigarette. And then she winks at him.

CHAPTER 5

NOW

A pack of razor blades, unopened.

Jon has finished his magic show at the club, to raucous applause. He didn't see her during the performance but Emily is in the crowd, in some fancy, cream bodice-hugging Victorian dress she no doubt has pilfered from a museum. He finishes puking into the toilet in the back room and pauses in the bathroom. The thin walls are covered in graffiti and he can hear people discussing how he pulled off his tricks.

"It's a series of lasers and Kerako® Tangi-Surfaces, the whole place is rigged with them and all he does is trigger them off a standard midi-controller he has sewn into the inside of his clothing. There's obviously also some kind of hallucinogen in the drinks or pumped through the vents. Simple really," says the disembodied voice.

Jon allows himself a smile. They have no idea just how simple it is. He comes out the side entrance, wearing a black shirt and jacket, blue denim jeans; different clothes so that fewer people will recognise him from the stage. Emily knows this is where he escapes from and runs up to him and hugs him because no matter how many times she sees his illusions, she's still impressed every time. And she knows that what he has to feel to make it all work kills him a little inside, even if he won't let on. Some part of her wonders how much of him is left to kill but she doesn't say it. She never says it.

"Hey, sexy lady." One of the drunk patrons bumps into her, his lower face green with absinthe and his eyes wild from something else. She brushes him off with practiced ease.

"Don't ignore me, bitch. You wouldn't want to ignore me," says the fat, filthy random. He comes back for more and now his hands are on her breasts while she's trying to shove him away. He's leering at her, ignoring Jon, who is at this very second standing right beside her.

Jon doesn't mind what other people do to him. Other people are scum and he does his best to ignore them and let them happen to themselves. But now, someone is bothering Emily and Emily is one of the two people in the world who actually matter to him. For a moment, this dirty, drunk fool has broken something inside Jon and he doesn't hold back. For someone who has trouble getting along with people or knowing how to interact with them, Jon knows a surprising amount about how their minds work and how to break them. He grabs the swaying drunk by the jacket and pulls him close, then grabs his wrist and twists it. Jon uses his other hand to grab the guy's head and whips it back, whispering in his ear, "You should kill yourself."

"Ge'off, go do some fucking card tricks and leave me and the lady alone!" yells the punter. Jon keeps whispering and the whispering gets faster and faster in the man's ear.

"I will, but before I do, I need you to remember to kill yourself. Seriously. Kill yourself. Later on, when this is over, you'll be wondering what I hoped to accomplish by telling you this. What I wanted to accomplish is this: I want you to really, seriously consider killing yourself. And every time you stop yourself and think that it's silly, when you're seriously asking yourself, 'Why the hell would I want to kill myself?' I want you to ask yourself. 'Why not?' I want the thought to slowly sneak its way back into your mind when you try to sleep tonight. Note that I said try. Because you won't be able to. The idea of killing yourself will slowly become more and more real until it becomes not an idea but an inevitability. And if you don't kill yourself tonight by some small miracle, then when you wake up, as you're making breakfast and nursing your hangover, replaying the night's events in your mind, the idea of taking a steak knife to your own throat will pop up. You can pretend it won't, but we both know it will, just because I'm saying it, just because you're thinking of it right now. Right now. Tomorrow morning. Every night and every morning until you end your miserable, pathetic existence. A man becomes his thoughts and these are now yours. I give them to you. Now run away."

The punter's eyes glass over and he struggles, trying to get away from Jon. Jon lets go and lets him fall to the floor. He knows he shouldn't have done that but the post-performance rush messes with his head. He needs to calm down. He needs more Sadness. He pushes through the circle that's gathered around him and grabs Emily by the hand to take her with him.

"I can take care of myself, Jon," says Emily and she whips her hand out of his.

"A simple thank you will suffice," says Jon. Sometimes he understands everything and sometimes, he understands nothing.

"You shouldn't have done that," says Emily.

"I didn't realise you were into drunk assholes these days, Emily."

"Is he really going to kill himself? Can you make him do that?"

"I don't know. Maybe," says Jon. "He deserved it."

"For what? For touching my boobs? You're going to make a man kill himself for touching my fucking boobs?"

"Oh no! Someone's going to die! Considering everyone who's died, do you really think that guy matters, Emily? Do you really and honestly care?" Emily pointedly ignores him. There's no reasoning with him when he's like this. He walks off into the night. Emily doesn't go after him. She knows where he'll be later on. On her front doorstep. Begging for another hit of Sadness.

Sure enough, like clockwork, when she gets home, he's already there, in the marbled archway, waiting for her.

"Go home to Michelle," says Emily.

"I can't yet, I just need a little—" says Jon.

"No, you don't, Jon. You don't need anything, least of all more Sadness. It's messing with you. You've always been quiet and sarcastic but now you're quiet and sarcastic and mean. I used to feel sorry for you," says Emily.

"I know. I'm sorry, Emily. Please. I can change," says Jon. She can't tell if he's making fun of her when he says, "I can change," as dramatically as he does. But of course, she lets him in again and he falls again and like every other time, he takes part of her with him.

Later, when he's leaving, he thinks for a moment that she doesn't even charge him for the Sadness anymore. He forgets to pay, a lot. He forgets a lot of things, a lot. He struggles, trying to feel bad for the situation he's put her in but can't. He's walking down the stairs and then everything goes black. The memory gap stretches from outside Emily's apartment to when he's back on the steam train, wearing headphones plugged into the train's music box without any sound playing through them, just to stop people from trying to talk to him, just in case any-one tries. He knows silence is best afterwards. There are always one or two people who take too much from him and he always finds them at performances like that one. The fight with the drunk and Emily also drained him. The train stops at a red light and a neighbourhood Peace Patrol carriage stops next to the train. He doesn't look, even when the mechanical horse flares exhaust fumes out of its nostrils.

The Peace Patrol carriage seems to be the last excessive machine on Earth. The Peace Ambassadors don't have to deal with technology ra-tions like the rest of the populace and so only they can make something as garish as this: a steel, ornate carriage, filled to the brim with the latest tech and weaponry, capable of carrying up to six fully-armed Ambas-sadors inside and a richly and intricately carved, armour-plated exterior. Then there was the horse. The mechanical horse that pulled the car-riage, also loaded with weapons, was its own entity, verging on having independent thought but still subservient to the driver of the carriage.

Jon does his best to continue not looking and instead focuses on the giant shifting flashboard across the street. Sensing that his eyes have re-mained fixed on the image for more than three seconds, the flashboard sends the sound directly into his ears.

"Are you or someone you know sad? Upset? Report them today to the United Government for re-inspiration! Win cool prizes!"

There's a boiling pot of paranoia in the pit of his stomach. That slow, heavy weight he always has when he leaves the house, when he's in the open and he's carrying something, even if it's just one vial of Sadness. He feels vulnerable. He knows if they stop him or the train, they'll search everyone and give all of them a hard time.

He just wants to get home without trouble. That's all he's ever want-ed. To ignore the rest of the world, enjoy the Sadness, eat and sleep and be with Michelle. If they give him a hard time, they'll search him. And if they search him, they'll find Sadness on him and then there'll be hell to pay.

He tries desperately to remember if this has happened before, if maybe he's really just back in bed with Michelle and this is all some immersive illusion of his own design. His mind plays tricks on him, maybe this is one of them. Please let this not be real. The Peace Ambassadors would love the fact that he was on Sadness. They'd howl as they beat him. The passenger window of the patrol carriage comes down smoothly, slowly, electrically and Jon can't help himself: he looks. It must be nice not to have technology rations. Even though there's no music playing on the steam train's music box, he feels the urge to turn it down. One of the bastards in the carriage waves at him and Jon's blood turns to ice water.

The Peace Ambassador asks the train driver to open up the train doors over a loudspeaker and the train driver, being a responsible citizen, does. It's not like he can do much about it; they could, if they wanted to, just disable the train remotely. The small vial of Saudade that Emily gave him as he left her apartment burns in his pocket. It's all he can think of. He can try and hide it but they'll probably radar/DNA sweep the train and find it and his DNA is all over it and they're so close now he can't risk just throwing it out the window, they'll have a camera on him. His only hope is that they don't bother searching him. One of the Peace Ambassadors is waiting by the carriage while the other one is inside. The one outside is staring right at Jon or at least that's what it feels like; Jon can't tell because of his bulletproof smiley face mask, created to hide their identities. It reminds him of the old Nirvana logo. Maybe someone at the club ratted him out, maybe Steve the half-ent or one of the poor kids in Tru-Sights™. Maybe Barnston, that top-hatted bastard. The government pays good money for information. Maybe he's going to be sent back to the camp where they cut your tattoos off. He can hear heavy footsteps coming down the hallway outside. The door to his cabin opens and groans under the weight forcing it back.

"Good evening, sir! We'd like to scan your arm and check your briefcase if that's ok with you." The mechanical voice box crackles around the Peace Ambassador's neck as he speaks, giving the speaker a Stephen Hawking accent, disguising his voice like the brutally simple smiley mask disguises his face.

"Go right ahead, sir," says Jon, standing up and stepping away from the briefcase.

Smiling, Shit-Eating Grin, as Jon decides to name him, politely tells him what he's going to do and even makes it feel like he has a choice in the matter. He knows there's nothing on his record, he's managed to avoid getting caught for anything too serious over the years and there's nothing but sandwiches in the suitcase, but if they search him, they'll find the Saudade and that'll mean trouble. Big trouble.

"Where have you been tonight, sir?" asks Shit-Eating Grin, almost cheerfully.

"Cabaret du Néant. Over on Friedman Drive," says Jon.

There's no point in lying. He can hear the second Peace Ambassador in the carriage outside speaking to whomever controls these assholes and going through a GPS tracker in the car, confirming his whereabouts by tracing the chip in his arm.

"I hear they sometimes have people getting weepy, getting a bit sad, that sort of thing, if you know what I mean," says Shit-Eating Grin.

"I wouldn't know, it's the first time I've been there," says Jon.

This is his first lie of the evening. There's no going back now.

"Is that so, sir?" asks Shit-Eating Grin, folding his arms behind his back.

"Yip."

"And this, this is your briefcase sir?" asks Shit-Eating Grin. He taps the briefcase with his fingers. The armoured suit he is wearing make his actions seem exaggerated, almost comical.

"Yip," says Jon.

Shit-Eating Grin opens it. Jon doesn't know how, but he knows that he's smiling under that fucking smiley face mask.

"So these are your vials of Sadness then, sir?" asks Shit-Eating Grin. He spins the suitcase around. It's filled with vials of Sadness, neatly stacked next to each other in rows.

"No, no, those aren't mine, that's got to be the wrong briefcase," says Jon, stepping away and raising his hands. "I'm not even lying this time, that's not mine."

Jon is hoping against hope that this is part of some grand delusion. Some bad trip. Maybe he's still in bed with Michelle. But he recognises the bitter aftertaste of reality.

"Your attitude is noted for future reference. What's also interesting sir, is that according to our navigation unit records and your train pass, you've been to the Cabaret du Néant once a week, every week, for the past year, give or take a month," says Shit-Eating Grin.

When the citizens of a place become the sport of those in authority, it is not a good place to be. Without warning, Shit-Eating Grin shoves his hands into Jon's pockets and he can feel his fat, gloved fingers closing around the glass vial. That's all they need. They'll never believe anything he says now. Not that they would, anyway. There's a violent release of serotonin and his body's chemicals wash him in strange relief. He doesn't have to worry about it being found anymore, because it's been found. Now, only the worst can happen, and he is sure of that. There is peace in his sureness of the events to follow. He knows now, he'll die.

Sure enough, twenty minutes later he's handcuffed to a chair in a small room and another man is hitting him in the face, repeatedly.

CHAPTER 6

THEN

On a distant battlefield, somewhere in the Middle East, Sergeant Jackson is sick of this fucking war and stands up from behind the trench he's hiding in, ignores the pleas of his squad mates to get down and starts to play the electric guitar he's insisted he bring into battle with him. He plays a song: his father's favourite. He's spent years learning it and he thinks it's beautiful. The first bullet kills him. Someone takes a picture as he falls. A dying soldier clutching his electric guitar.

The wink from Michelle creates a fracture in Jon's heart.

"What's wrong with you, Michelle? Stop lying," says Emily.

"What are you talking about, Emily? Of course I love comic books, I always have," she laughs.

Emily shakes her head and looks away. Jon might not be her best friend but she doesn't like anyone making fun of him. She turns to him when her popular friends turn on her and she doesn't want to lose that sanctuary. He may be a bit of a dork sometimes but he's her dork. The cicadas continue to serenade the three of them, unaware of teenage politics.

"So, what do you read?" Jon finally asks.

"All sorts of stuff," says Michelle, giggling to herself.

"I got a new one today, it's a special limited edition copy of *The Black Kracken* with a silver foil cover where they reveal where the space ship comes from," says Jon, leaning forward as he says it.

"Really?" asks Michelle, her eyes dramatically wide.

"Yip, I've got it at home," says Jon. He is proud of this. He has never been able to be proud of a comic book before but he is now.

This moment stretches out before he says, "I could show it to you. You could borrow it I mean."

"When?" asks Michelle and she stops swinging.

"Tonight, if you'd like, if you guys don't have anything better to do," says Jon. He digs his fingernails into his palm.

They all look at each other, amongst the old beams supporting the swings, near the jungle gym and the slide and under this moon.

Emily bites her lip. Michelle is cool. Emily can be cool, too. She just needs to let Michelle have her fun with Jon. It's ok she decides. Jon's a dork, not a pussy, not some fragile little flower. It'd even do him good to get hurt a little.

"Well, I'm sleeping at Emily's house tonight, so she can leave a door open for me and I'll come over and check out your comic book," says Michelle, turning to Jon and walking closer to him.

"Ok," says Jon, not quite sure anything like this is ever supposed to be this easy; but maybe that's how you knew you were with the one you were meant to be with. Maybe it was always easy.

The blood is pumping hot in his ears. They put out their cigarettes; they've smoked them to the filter and the head rush leaves all three of them feeling dizzy. They slowly get up off the swings and leave them swaying in the gentle summer breeze. The smell of the blooming flowers around them is still strong in the air.

The trip back to his house, even though it's only maybe a hundred steps away, feels longer and some part of him knows he must now make stilted, casual conversation. He must be smooth.

"Do you read any other titles?" Jon asks.

"Yes, a bunch," says Michelle.

Emily grabs Michelle by the arm and viciously whispers something in her ear and Michelle shakes her off and starts walking faster, still giggling.

"This is where I leave you. Don't be back too late, Michelle," says Emily, as they get to Jon's house and she and Michelle exchange a look. But she keeps walking towards her house, just on the other side of Blakefield Avenue.

"You sure you don't want us to walk you there?" Jon asks. It's one of the safest neighbourhoods in the city but there's some kind of safety line that Emily offers and he's not sure he really wants to cut it.

"No, I'll be ok, you guys have fun," says Emily and she turns and she disappears slowly into the night, step by soft step, into the silence.

Jon and Michelle stand in the gravel driveway. He glances over at a spot in the gravel where he cut his foot open as a child, on some green broken glass from a discarded beer bottle. He still has the scar.

"Are you ok with coming?" Jon asks. He feels stupid and nervous and he's getting sick and tired of the voice in his head screaming: "RE-LAX! JUST RELAX! JUST! RELAX!"

"Sure," she replies with a smile and she closes her eyes slightly when she says it. Jon feels less stupid and less nervous. He pats his pockets where he always keeps the key for the front door. It isn't there. There is only air and nothingness where the key should be. Michelle cannot see Jon's face in the moonlight, otherwise she would notice how pale he's suddenly become.

"What's wrong?" asks Michelle.

"Nothing, just hold on," says Jon. She rubs her arms. It isn't cold.

"It has to be here somewhere," says Jon. Jon pats his pockets again, even though it isn't going to magically appear on a second search but he hopes against hope that, somehow, it does. It doesn't.

"Can you wait here? I need to get into the house from the back and then I'll come and unlock here," he asks.

"If that's what you've got to do," says Michelle with a sigh.

"It'll only take a second," says Jon. He's not very convincing. In truth, he has no idea how he's going to get back into the house but he has to try. By all that is holy, he has to try.

"Ok then, hurry up," says Michelle.

She rubs her arms again. It still isn't cold.

Jon runs through the front yard, to the side gate at the edge of the house and scrambles over it, pushing his feet into the gaps between the rails to hoist himself up and over, before making his way through his family's small backyard to the sliding door. It had locked behind him when he went through it. But there's a window open near it that, only a few years before, he'd been able to squeeze through, if he got in at just the right angle. He's stockier now, just after the end of childhood, but only slightly, and he has to try. He moves a paint can under the window and stands on it to reach the burglar bars, which he uses to pull himself up onto the sill.

He manages to squeeze his head through and then the light in the room turns on and he hears a voice.

"Jon?" says Jon's father.

All of Jon's hopes have left him. Some part of him is glad that his father is so used to him sneaking out at night that he doesn't mistake him for a burglar and shoot him. The rest of him is bitterly disappointed.

"It's me."

"What are you doing?"

"I just wanted to…to get some air."

"Ah yes, air. I always climb in through the window when I want air. Speaking of which, why are you climbing through the window?" asks Jon's father.

"No reason," says Jon.

Jon's father doesn't say anything for a moment before finally speaking, "Just try not to make too much noise."

"Yes, Dad. Thanks, Dad," says Jon.

"Get inside," says Jon's father.

He unlocks the door and lets him in. He has a funny expression on his face like he knows more than what's been let on and he ruffles his son's short hair. Jon shakes his father's hand off. He can do nothing at this point except retreat to his bedroom. He's glad at least that his father caught him and not his mother. His mother's always on edge. She always seems like the world is too much for her; luckily Jon has inherited none of her high-strung nature. Jon turns the light off and goes to the window and pulls back the curtains, also covered with comic book characters, to tell Michelle what's happened and give her the comic he's promised her: *The Black Kracken* special edition that she seemed so interested in. He'll explain what happened and they'll see each other again tomorrow, once his tests are finished. He scans the darkness for her. She's not there, not hiding in the bushes, nothing. She's gone. He knows she's gone.

"Michelle?" Jon whispers into the night.

No response.

Jon will find the key in his box of cigarettes tomorrow morning.

CHAPTER 7

NOW

A man looks down at the red paint on his hands and wonders for a moment if he's killed his wife and this is her blood or maybe he's just painted the garden bench red, that's all. He thinks it is a strange thought and carries on digging the hole he's digging in the back garden. He whistles. He writes this all down in his moleskin diary, later that evening. His wife should be back from work by now but she isn't.

Somewhere else, Jon shifts against the handcuffs holding him in the painfully hard wooden chair in the small interrogation room, trying to find some kind of comfortable position. There isn't one.

Jon decides to call this Peace Ambassador "Deformed," as that name is as good as any. He's taken off the smiling, bulletproof face mask and has a scar across his face and Jon wishes he'd given it to him. Deformed seems resigned to the fact, if not happy about it, that he's going to have to hurt someone and that someone is Jon.

"I wouldn't have to use the fucking drugs if you'd stop drugging the water supply. Besides, that briefcase wasn't mine and you guys know it, my briefcase had sandwiches in it and no amount of bullshit is going to change that."

For the most part, Deformed ignores him and paces up and down, then he sits down and folds his hands in front of him and says, "Doing what you're doing, using this Sadness shit, this…garbage, romanticising it, you're not making friends with us or anyone else in the United

Government. Why? Why bring this on?"

"Because 'fuck you' is why," says Jon. The United Government. That must be where he is. He's in the tall white spires where they take political and emotional prisoners and their families or friends for reconditioning. Michelle. Oh God, Michelle. Where's Michelle? Is she here?

Bang. *Now's not the time, Jon*, some far off voice tells him. *Think about yourself for a second, forget about Michelle.* Deformed slams his fist into Jon's face again and Jon can feel some of his teeth losing their grip. All the stars come out to play in front of his eyes. Blood pours from his mouth in a steady torrent.

"I'm sorry, citizen, I didn't quite catch that, could you repeat yourself?" says Deformed.

"My apologies, officer, your fist was in my face," says Jon under his breath. Jon is somewhere else right now. Please leave a message after the bang. Bang. Jon is pretty sure that this is what it feels like to go completely insane. Not just partially. Completely.

"Because your mother is a whore," says Jon.

Now Jon does something he's promised himself he'll never do: he uses his gift in front of a Peace Ambassador, the gift his father never got the chance to explain to him, the one he had to discover himself. The air thins and the light around both of them seems to shiver and it slowly pulls together into a humanoid shape.

Jon thinks of his friend James. Sweet, gentle James. He was like a brother to him. And now he imagines, no, he remembers what it was like to see James burning on that cross, what it was like to see him reduced to cinders when they threw him from that plane, covered in liquid magnesium. He imagines the sky burial of his almost-brother, James.

It hurts so much to see him but he doesn't care. Deformed, because he doesn't have a brother, sees his sister. He sees his sister burning alive.

"Whoa, what are you doing?" asks Deformed.

Jon forces himself to imagine James burning in unforgiving detail and the smell of burning flesh fills the room. The Peace Ambassador sees his sister burning, burning, burning. After opening and closing his mouth a few times like a goldfish, he looks from Jon to his sister, then back again. He starts to scream, a low, steadily rising noise. Then his fist finds Jon's face again. Bang. Bang. Bang. Bang. Bang. The illusion flickers with each blow, like someone hitting a TV set too hard. Jon spits out what's left of his teeth.

And with his last moments of consciousness, he says quietly, "Because you've made sadness a disease, you fucking loser. Happiness without sadness is emptiness, nothingness. The world once taught us to say, 'I'm sorry,' when we still cried, as if what we were doing was something to be ashamed of. What you've done is worse."

Deformed, sweating from the sheer effort of the beating, manages to smile through his teeth even though his sister is still in the room, burning alive. Now she's looking at him. She mouths the words, "I miss you."

Deformed leans on Jon's neck and says, "I want you to be happy. The world wants you to be happy." He flexes one of his arms and cracks his already bloody knuckles.

"…Then why does it have to get so goddamn angry at me, when I'm not?"

"Stop it. Stop it. STOP IT." Deformed screams.

Bang.

Jon passes out and things stop making sense. At no point in his entire life has he ever considered his life normal. Occasionally stable perhaps, but never normal. And if you accept the fact that everyone gets what they want in the end, one way or another, then you also have to accept the fact that right now, whatever you're doing, however you're feeling, you're getting what you want. Jon's father told him that. Dad?

Emily's voice carries on behind him, then seems to leave her mouth and follow him through the house, his parents' house. It sticks to him like a living thing, crawling over his arms and up his shoulders, seeping into his ears, "Don't wind up like him Jon. Don't wind up like your father."

Everything is a mist.

When he comes to, there's a gnarled figure standing over him, pouring water over his face. His natural reaction to lash out at him is tempered by the fact that he is in no way guaranteed, by the looks of his host, that he will get a second punch.

Host is the wrong word; they're both guests of the state. After blinking some of the water out of his eyes and getting a glimpse of his surroundings, he finds himself in pain in a small, grey, concrete room with a low ceiling. The room is empty, save for his fellow guest, a bucket of water, the ladle inside it, and a second, thankfully emptier bucket.

"Who are you and what do you want?" says his fellow occupant.

"I'm Jon," says Jon.

"I'm Edward. Semi-professional human hater…and eater," says Edward.

"Your name is Edward Eta?" asks Jon, forgetting the pain and confusion for a moment.

"No you stupid…eater…I eat humans," says Edward.

That's what he hasn't been able to put his finger on: he's sharing his cell with a half-ent. His fellow guest taps his whirled chin as if he's thinking. It sounds like a great break on a snooker table. Leaves flow like dreadlocks from his head.

"No offense, but you can't be too good at your job if your job is eating people and you helped me," says Jon.

"Helped you?" asks Edward.

"You threw water in my face," says Jon.

"I like to make sure whatever I'm going to eat isn't alive when I do it. And if you were dead, the water would wash some of those heal bots off of your face. It's a courtesy I may start forgetting one of these days," says Edward.

Jon knows he's lying. The rumours of half-ents eating humans are nothing but urban legends, started by panicky housewives soon after The End when the half-ents showed up. That on its own isn't reason enough to test his luck. He shivers slightly as he realises that everything hasn't been a bad dream. They put the heal bots, tiny particle-sized electromechanical medic machines, on him as soon as he passed out. He can feel his teeth back in his mouth, shiny and new.

"Still, thank you," says Jon.

Edward sighs and says, "Don't worry about it. You'll have bigger problems soon enough, same's me."

"What's your deal?"

"What do you mean?"

"I mean why are you in this cell?"

"I'm in this cell because the current government doesn't seem to take kindly to people campaigning for recognition and the right to vote, even if you happen to be a tree."

"You're an activist?"

"No, worse. A sentient creature, something with consciousness that wants to have the same rights as people who don't look like trees."

"So you started a riot or something?"

"Worse. I handed out pamphlets."

"How is a pamphlet worse than a riot?"

"Because words are forever. Even if you kill the person who writes them, words are forever. Even if you disagree with them and spend the rest of your days arguing against what was said, what was said was still said. A riot only lasts as long as it takes for a fire to burn itself out."

Jon nodded. Great. A political tree with a penchant for rabble-rousing.

"And you?" asks Edward.

"I was framed."

"That's original."

"I was only half arrested for the right reason."

"What is the right reason to be arrested?"

"The right reason, or at least the legal and official reason I was arrested, was for possession of Sadness. But they planted some on me, too."

"You're a junkie?" Edward recoiled slightly and a shadowed expression passed quickly across his face like a summer storm.

"No, I'm normal. I take the Sadness to counteract the shit the government puts in the water supply."

"Oh, really?"

"Yes, really."

"That's bullshit. You're a fucking junkie."

"I don't drink, I don't do cocaine, I don't shoot heroin, I just take Sadness."

"You can try and justify it however you want but the point is, you're a slave to something. Something else is in control of you and when that happens, you can either fight it or ignore it or try to justify it, or you can do what you're doing, which is try to make it make sense. That's what you're doing."

"Who the fuck are you to lecture me?" asks Jon, forgetting just how big the person he's just met is.

The conversation is cut short as the door to the cell opens with a dull, ominous clank.

Two Peace Ambassadors come into the room, one after the other. They stand on either side of the door, in a manner that suggests that a third person will soon be coming through it. When he does, Jon has an instant dislike for the white-haired, scraggily-bearded man that eventually steps out of the shadows and into the room. He's wearing a white lab coat with numerous pens sticking out of the pocket and thick-rimmed glasses. He looks like a doctor. Jon will call him the doctor.

"Good evening, gentlemen," says the doctor.

"Fuck you," spits Edward.

"I understand your anger," says the doctor and it doesn't even sound like he's being condescending.

Edward sighs and leans back. He has a collar around his neck that Jon suspects is weakening him; there is little else to explain the fact that the half-ent hasn't launched himself up and at the trio in front of them.

"Jon, I'd like a word with you. Edward, some of my colleagues would like to talk to you about the political flyers you've been printing and handing out," says the doctor.

"They have a problem with philosophy?"

"I believe they have a problem with certain subversive ideas you're promoting."

"So that's a yes then."

"You'll see them soon, you can ask them yourself. You are not under my department's jurisdiction," the doctor turns and smiles at Jon. "He however, is."

Both of them are dragged by the guards from where they were on the floor through the dirty passage that runs between the cells. There's Harkan™ Clean Sweeps installed on either end of the passage, machines designed to automatically sanitise an area; so it's obvious, Jon thinks, that the guards leave the corridor filthy on purpose.

"Take Edward to the committee for rebuilding and reworking," says the doctor.

"So they can make a coffee table out him?" asks the shorter of the two guards. It's always the little ones who say the most.

"No, Ivan, treat our guests properly," says the doctor.

"Your mother was poison ivy and your father was fertilizer," says Edward. The bigger guard slams his gun into the back of Edward's head.

"Jon is going to my office," says the doctor.

The other guard lets out a grunt and drags Jon by the shirt behind them, who is now barely struggling. Now Jon's wondering if he'll ever see Michelle again. Perhaps they will experiment on him before they kill him. They lead him into a lift; the doctor obviously has his own. As they go up, the windows flash by and Jon gets a glimpse of NewLand. The floating news zeppelin constantly hovering above the city relays a headline about a terrorist captured on a train. There's a picture of Jon. He focuses on the news screen and waits for the audio to be beamed into his head but it isn't. It's the glass; he supposes the United Government building doesn't handle audio feeds too well. Intentionally probably. Jon tries to see if he can spot Emily's apartment or his own. Maybe he'll see Michelle in the window but he can't; everything is too far away.

They drag him out the lift and down another passageway, past several laboratories and one particularly strange room with thick black velvet curtains and a series of mechanical sextants, powered by massive fires, and they whir as they track the stars. They take him through plain, white, and unassuming plastic doors. The white-haired doctor's office is made of a kind of chrome and wood hybrid that reflects strange silver patterns of light, which are coming from what looks to be a real WindowSkreen™ (not a recording), a literal window into the past, currently set to a field in France during a particular bloody revolution. Cannons fire and men die silently behind the glass. Tomorrow, the same day will replay itself but perhaps in a different location, depending on what model it is. The windows make up the majority of decor in the room, which is otherwise a very clean, white space, except for a cluttered oak desk. The guard shoves him into a lush, leather chair in front of the desk and Jon offers no resistance. They activate two cuffs on the armrests and Jon is restrained.

The white-haired doctor enters the room from a door at the back of the office and sits down in a second leather chair on the opposite side of the desk, facing Jon.

The man Jon has never met before in his life says, "Your father was a great man."

CHAPTER 8

THEN

A lady practices falling down so that her abusive, amnesiac husband will think he's already beaten her and just leave her the hell alone. She keeps a secret video log of all that happens, miles away.

Jon is lying in bed, still unable to sleep, still with a test to write to-morrow. He thinks of Michelle, of the way her body moved on the swing at the park, of the sound of her voice; he thinks of his comic books, of *The Black Kracken*, of what the heroes he reads about would do in this situation. He's angry at Michelle for leaving and not waiting for the comic book and he's angry with his father for screwing with his plans to get Michelle inside the house. He's angry with him in the way that only people close to you are allowed to be angry with you. Jon sits up in his bed. He's never been so close to being alone with a girl. God-fucking-damn-it. He gets out of bed and slowly but purposefully punches the wall with a dull thud, then collapses and starts to cry softly to himself.

"Stop being such a pussy," he says out aloud and only to himself.

He thinks of how strong and confident the characters in his comic books are.

Suddenly, bright light fills the room. He can tell because the backs of his eyes turn red and he thinks someone's heard him, mom or dad, and they've turned the bedroom light on but this is brighter than the bedroom light.

This is brighter than daylight.

Jon can feel the air becoming thinner and there's less of it than there was seconds before. Jon can sense something behind him, something eating the shadows around him. He turns his head slowly and very carefully, he opens his eyes. It's hard to focus on at first but a being, a creature made of pure white light, is now in the room with Jon. Jon's eyes are as open as they'll ever be and all the air has left his lungs, burnt up by the light. There's so much of it. They must be able to see this light out in space. As his brain finally catches up with what's happening, he tries to open his mouth to scream but he can't. He's frozen in place. The being is holding a lance made of pure, white light and has muscles twice the size of its head. It's every comic book hero Jon has ever read about, ever dreamed, on fire, all at once. The being opens its mouth; flames lick its lips and dance across what looks like ancient armour.

"It's all going to be ok," it says.

Jon, finally, manages to close his eyes and yell, scream, make some kind of guttural sound and as he does, the being disappears. There's a giant 'whoomp' noise, like the biggest candle in the world has just been blown out. The lights go on in the house.

The bedroom door bursts open. Jon's father stands in the doorway with the gun he normally keeps in the safe. Jon is on the floor. His knuckles are bleeding from where he's punched the wall. His face is ashen and his eyes are red. Jon's father kneels down next to him and grabs him by the shoulders.

"What's wrong? What happened?" says Jon's father.

"Da-dad," says Jon.

"What happened?" repeats his father, scanning the room desperately, looking for whomever or whatever attacked his son.

"There was…there was something," says Jon.

"What?"

"I—I don't know."

"What did you see?"

"I saw…I saw a man made of light."

Jon's father's eyes betray too much. He's taking this seriously. Jon does not expect that. Jon believes one of them may have gone insane. Perhaps both of them. Perhaps this is a dream.

"Were you thinking about him before you saw him?"

"Not him in particular, comic books, *The Black Kracken*." Jon's father nods at this.

"Where were you tonight? Were you with a girl? I heard girls' voices outside your bedroom window earlier, Jon, don't lie to me."

"I—I…yes," says Jon.

Jon's father sighs. He holds Jon. Jon's brain is on fire. He holds him tighter.

"So, it's genetic then and it's happening to you, too," says Jon's father under his breath.

"What do you mean?"

"This is hard to explain, but I started to see similar things when I was a child."

"That doesn't make any sense."

"The first thing you should know is that what gives it power is what you think of. You need to be careful of what you think of." .

"I don't understand."

"I think of the things that protect you. I think of the oak tree outside and your space ninjas from that comic book you bury your head in."

"They're space pirates, Dad, not ninjas."

"It doesn't matter, what matters is that I think of the things that protect you and as you get older, that will become more and more important."

"This is crazy."

"I need you to trust me and go to sleep."

"Go to sleep? Go to fucking sleep?" asks Jon. Jon doesn't believe he will ever be able to sleep again.

"I'm letting you use that language with me because you're in shock. Now pay attention, I can tell you about what's happened, I can explain everything but I need you to go to sleep right now and let me try and work out what to do."

Jon is helped back to bed. Jon's father leaves the room and comes back with a pill. He gives it to Jon and holds him while he falls asleep.

Jon does not dream. When he wakes up, his father's pocket watch is clasped tightly in his hand.

CHAPTER 9

NOW

The last poet in the world writes words on rocks with thick black permanent marker then dives to the bottom of the crystal water in the bay of NewLand and arranges them. He will never tell anyone what the poem says and the only people who'll ever be able to read it are the ones who can dive as deep as he once did.

Jon is convinced at this point that there is no reason for the government's sadism, that it's all just the fun and games of those in power and that they do it simply because they can. Why else would "Dr. Herengracht," according to the little sign on his desk, tell him he knew his father?

"I believe you know my father in the same way I believe that my suitcase was filled with vials of Sadness when the Peace Ambassadors picked me up in the train."

The doctor smiles. "That was an unfortunately necessary aspect of our plan to get you here. Apparently it wasn't even needed; you had a vial of Sadness in your pocket."

"What do you want with me? Where's Michelle?"

"Michelle? Your girlfriend. She's an incredibly interesting phenomenon. Almost as interesting as the relationship between you and your father, Jon Salt." No one's used Jon's surname in years and the name sounds strange when he hears it now.

"She's a person, not a phenomenon. Leave Michelle out of this." The doctor smiles.

"Fine. Let's talk about your father, Peter Salt."

"What do you know about my father?"

"Your father used to work for me."

"Bullshit. My father was an engineer."

"Yes, that's what he told his family and friends because that was the requirement for working on the projects he worked on with me, exploring his gifts. The same gifts you have, apparently," says the doctor, folding his hands.

"There's no way my father worked for the government. This government, this global institution of leaders or United Government whatever the hell you want to call it is evil and you, you and people like you, have fucked the world. He was a good man. A better man than you'll ever be."

"Ah, you are correct there, my friend," says the doctor. He goes to stand by the window and watches men from the past die through the WindowSkreen™.

"He did not work for this government. He worked for the previous government. And as you well know, the previous government became this government only after some very fundamental changes to it and the world," continued the doctor.

"He was killed in The End," Jon says more to himself than anyone else in the room. He hasn't talked about his father in a long time.

"Now you are incorrect, my friend. Your father was not killed in The End," says the doctor. Jon's muscles contract.

"What do you mean?" asks Jon. A spasm shoots through his body as he tries to launch himself out of the chair, some primal force driving him but the restraints hold him tight.

The doctor laughs. "You are quite the energetic one, my friend."

"I'm not your fucking friend," says Jon.

"No, but you will be. Take him away," says the doctor.

"Tell me about my father!" screams Jon as the guards come in. The doctor shakes his head and looks away.

"All in good time; but first, you need to calm down," says the doctor.

"You're a liar! You're a liar!" yells Jon as he's dragged out of the room.

The doctor, oblivious to the wild animal Jon has become, mumbles under his breath, "All in good time."

Jon is returned to the cell where he paces back and forth, thinking about what the doctor said. It can't be true. His father is dead. He know's he's dead. He felt something die inside him when The End happened. No, the doctor was only playing games with him. Messing with his head for the sake of messing with it. Jon tries to sleep. He doesn't. It's not the whir of the machines outside, it's the grinding of the gears inside his head. In the middle of the night, the guards throw open the door.

"Here's your friend, you freak," says Deformed.

A gasping mass of wood and sap is thrown into the cell with him. Edward. The guards slam the door shut and the rustling of leaves and shallow breathing is the only sound left. Jon quickly gets on the bucket of water and pulls some of the boarding off the cell window, letting the cold in but also some moonlight, enough to see Edward. Jon's heart almost stops. Edward's wooden body is covered in cuts and burns, thick gouts of sap weep from his wounds. He shouldn't be alive. He probably won't be for much longer. Thankfully, he's only barely conscious.

"What did they do to you?" asks Jon, stripping his shirt from his back to turn into make-shift bandages, forgetting that this is the same person who called him a junkie hours before.

"Only the things I'll be doing back to them soon," says Edward through what must be exquisite pain. Jon rolls him over to try and cover the worst of the wounds, which is when he sees that one of Edward's arms is gone; thin ribbons of wood are all that remain.

"Your arm, Edward, your arm…" says Jon.

"I know, son, it'll grow back," says Edward. He laughs and hacks up sap into his throat. Jon has never and will never meet a man or creature with the ability to laugh in the face of pain like Edward ever again. Jon shakes his head and continues to bandage him. It takes him more than an hour but most of Edward's more serious wounds are covered, even the stump that used to be his left arm.

"The bastards didn't even take my good one," says Edward and that's the last thing he says before his brown eyes close and he sleeps. Jon is almost thankful for the distraction, for something to take his mind off his father and what the doctor said. He too finally finds some sleep.

He's woken up by the same two guards, kicking his body.

CHAPTER 10

THEN

Two sets of initials in a heart, carved into the heart of
a tree more than 100 years old, grown over with bark,
keeping love a secret. Now hacked out of the wood.

Meanwhile, somewhere else in time, Jon is eating his breakfast.
"Where's Dad?" asks Jon.
"He went to work early. Why?" asks Jon's mother.
"No reason."
"You know you can talk to me, too."
"Uh-huh," Jon says, into his cereal. Maybe not about this. And besides, he's fallen into this trap before, he knows what happens: he tells her what's on his mind and the next minute he's in the shrink's office, having to explain why what's on his mind is on his mind. She made herself an alien. Not him.

He finishes his cereal, gets his bag and starts walking to school. He doesn't like school. He must hand in his recording for music class. He must write his test. He doesn't want to write his test. He just wants to be alone. He runs a stick along the side of the fence as he walks and it makes a click-clack sound. He just wants to see Michelle again. He loves her. He loves her like every mushy, romantic song he's ever heard has ever told him how to love someone.

Instead, the bells ring and he's late. He sprints around the corner, into the school playground and there's Gregory Ashcroft, resident asshole, who's good at sports and does fairly well academically. If you didn't talk to him, you'd say he was fairly good-looking but as soon as he opened his mouth, everything about him screamed asshole. Right now, for example, Justin Pearson, resident geek, who's not good at sports, kind of pale and doesn't do that well academically, is sitting down on the edge of the low wall in the playground at the front of the school, doing his best to ignore a crowd of children who have gathered around him and Gregory.

Gregory is saying, "Justin, if your parents had a little more money, you could go for plastic surgery, you know. You wouldn't have to live your life being ugly. Come on guys, let's start a collection for Justin's plastic surgery."

Gregory's cohorts and henchmen chortle to themselves and snigger at his unsurpassed, at least in their eyes, wit.

Jon knows he shouldn't be involved but fuck it.

"Yeah, Greg, but at least ugly can be fixed, stupid is forever." The playground laughs, hard, not at Justin anymore but at Gregory. Gregory slowly turns to Jon, his face red. He regains some of his composure by swallowing some air, at least by the looks of it, and stares straight at Jon before smiling and very slowly drawing his hand across his throat, like a blade. The message is unmistakable. Jon may have won the battle but the war is never ending. Fuck it. Justin, pale as he is, is a decent kid and doesn't deserve this kind of shit.

"You're all late!" comes the shrill voice from the entrance to the school and a teacher rings a bell, scowling at the children as they file past her.

Jon makes his way through the noise of the school halls to his first lesson, music class. Minutes after he enters, Jon's teacher has taken him outside. She has long, flowing black hair and Jon and every boy in the school has had a crush on her at one time or another. Each student was assigned the task of making a song. They could sing. They could play a guitar. They could run their finger over the lip of a glass. It didn't matter. It was supposed to be fun. Jon's recording is nothing but noise. Static. Thirty minutes of static. The kind you'd hear if you tuned the radio to a station that wasn't there.

"Why did you do this, Jon?" asks Jon's teacher.

"I thought we were allowed to do whatever we wanted," says Jon, kicking the ground.

"You were, but it had to be a song."

"It is a song," says Jon. He tries to get up and walk away, but she grabs his arm to stop him.

"Sit down, Jon. I'm your teacher, you're supposed to listen to me. This is really your idea of a song?"

"Yes."

"Ok, Jon. What are the words to your song?"

"They're whatever you want them to be."

"What do you mean?"

"I mean if you listen to it for long enough, you start to hear words." Jon's teacher is staring at him. Jon's teacher hasn't been trained for this.

"I made it white noise on purpose. That way, anyone could find what they were looking for in it."

"Go back inside and sit down," says Jon's teacher, sighing. She makes a note in a book. Jon's teacher doesn't know what to do. After music class, Jon is outside the school building five minutes before the start of his test and Gregory Ashcroft and several of his goons, including one who's particularly covered in acne, Jeremy Shaw, are slowly backing him into a corner by the lockers. Jon regrets nothing.

"What kind of retard makes a song out of noise?" says Gregory, slamming his fist into his open hand again and again.

"You're a bit of a freak, aren't you, Jonny boy?" asks Jeremy, who has the privilege of being Gregory's second in command. Jon turns around and faces the wall, not even acknowledging them. He'll just keep staring at the wall and they'll go away. Instead, it makes them angry.

"My name's Jon, not Jonny boy," says Jon quietly to the wall.

"What did you say, faggot?" asks Gregory.

One of the goons grabs Jon by the shoulders and shoves him towards Gregory. Gregory catches him with a fist in the stomach.

"Did that hurt? Jonny boy? Speak up, faggot," says Gregory.

Jon finds himself thinking of Michelle. The thought of Michelle makes him happy and he can feel the blood rushing through him in the same way it did the night before. Then he thinks of superheroes. He thinks of superheroes smashing through buildings, throwing cars. His mind takes him somewhere else. It tries to take him somewhere else. It doesn't quite work. Gregory is pulling Jon's hair. Tears are streaming down Jon's face. It hurts. This hurts. He wants to hurt them back. Suddenly, he feels Gregory's grip on his hair loosen and he hears Jeremy and the rest of his goons gasp.

"Look what you've done," whispers Jon.

He can feel the air thinning around him, like it did in his bedroom the night before. A giant creature made of fire and thorns looms over Jon, growing out of him, howling, clawing at the boys, reaching out for them. Gregory, Jeremy, and his friends run, screaming, not knowing or understanding what they're seeing. The monster becomes mist just as quickly as it became real but not before looking Jon straight in the eyes.

Jon sits in the corner, panting. Everything is red and he's covered in sweat and just as scared of himself as the other boys are. He just wants to be normal, but this sure isn't it. He still doesn't want to write his test and that at least, that not wanting to be at school, feels like it might be a normal thing to feel.

Jon, remembering what his father tells him about working hard and getting through things, remembering his father telling him that school doesn't last forever, walks towards the exam hall, trying to forget the monsters. None of it's real. None of it's real. None of it's real. He tries not to think about what's happened over the last twenty-four hours. He goes inside the hall, sits down and they hand out the paper. He takes out his pencil and tries to think of numbers, of how they fit together and he finds it hard. He'd find it hard even if things hadn't started jumping out of his head into the real world. He's good with words. Bad with numbers. Bad with directions. Good with pictures. He wonders if anyone is good at everything. He tries to stop wondering and focus on the test. The teacher, his music teacher, is walking up and down amongst the desks, moderating the test. Jon is pushing his pencil across the paper, across the symbols. Symbols that represent quantities of things. No specific things, just abstract things. That's what he finds difficult. Just things.

He tries to focus. He tries to drown out his thoughts. They cannot be drowned. They float to the surface. He's yelling at himself inside his head and just about to start crying when he feels a cold hand gripping his leg below the desk.

He freezes and looks down. A dark figure made of static and shadows is lying on the ground, staring up at him. The child behind him isn't in his desk anymore. No one else has seen the creature made of shadows gripping his leg. The hand slowly grips tighter and the dark figure starts to hiss. He thinks it's happening again, what happened the night before and with Gregory outside, it's happening again but it doesn't feel like him. This doesn't feel like him. He remembers what it felt like and something tells him he hasn't made this.

Someone else has made this, whatever it is. The shadow slowly starts trying to pull him from the chair. He grips onto the desk and holds on as tight as he can. A girl in the desk across looks up and sees what's happening and her faces freezes in pure fear. Jon looks at her, unable to scream, unable to do anything, holding on as tight as he can as the creature strains against him. She opens her mouth and screams for him. The silence in the hall is shattered and everyone turns as one. The figure leaps up and throws itself at the exam moderator, Jon's beautiful music teacher, tearing and ripping, blood spraying across the room in violent arcs. As if it were an encore of last night, bright light pours through the window, the air thins and everyone in the exam hall starts to scream louder, and then a blast wave hits and everything goes white.

CHAPTER 11

NOW

A fireman's axe, found in the ashes of a
burnt-out building.

"Look at that, the lovers have been cuddling," says Deformed.

"Put some clothes on, you freak," says the shorter one, the one who's quiet unless he's sure big Deformed is somewhere near. They throw a bright white jumpsuit at him and watch him get dressed. Edward's chest is rising and falling, which reassures Jon that he didn't die during the night, although the collar around his neck is still cutting into him, still making him weak.

"Don't worry, cupcake, we'll finish him off tonight," says Deformed. Jon looks away. He will not let them know he cares about anything anymore. They're just toying with him. Trying to make him snap. Fuck them.

"As for you, the doctor would like you to join him for breakfast. Now get up and walk or we'll drag you there like last time," says Deformed.

Jon gets up and follows them out, casting one last look at Edward before he leaves. He will be sad if he dies. They lead Jon through the twisting corridors of the compound and finally out onto a terrace, below the white marble spires. Waiting for him is a table made of the same wood and chrome hybrid from the doctor's office, two chairs, and plates stacked with food and a vase with a single red rose in it. The guards make Jon sit in the chair and fasten restraints around his arms.

The doctor walks in through a side door and says, "That won't be necessary, will it, Jon?"

Jon looks at him and then at the guards; he nods in agreement and the guards, after a confirming glance at the doctor, undo the restraints.

"How did you think he was going to eat?" asks the doctor. The guards shrug and slink off, leaving the two of them alone.

"You want to know about your father, don't you, Jon?" asks the doctor.

Jon doesn't trust his voice, so he just nods.

"We'll get to that soon enough. First, let's talk about what you did to one of the guards during your acquisition. He nearly went mad. We had to send men out in the middle of the night to find his sister and assure him that she wasn't anywhere near the cell you were in," says the doctor.

Jon chuckles to himself. It felt good to do that to the guard, even though it killed him inside to see James again. It was worth it.

"Tell me about that," says the doctor.

"Why should I?"

"You will if you want to know what happened to your father," says the doctor. There's a noticeable look of pain on Jon's face.

"I can see that got to you. If you want to know how he died, you'll cooperate," says the doctor. "I don't want to be mean but I will get what I need." The doctor loads his own plate with food.

"You were lying then, when you said I was wrong, that he didn't die in The End," Jon blurts out before remembering himself.

"I wasn't lying. He didn't die in The End. He died causing The End," says the doctor and he says it while cutting his eggs and bacon, like he's discussing the score from a sporting fixture, like he's talking about a traffic jam or the weather.

Jon remains still, not touching his food, wondering if it's as poisoned as the doctor's words, although if they were going to kill him, they would have just done it by now.

"You don't believe me?" asks the doctor.

Of course he's lying but Jon figures he might as well get a free breakfast out of it. He starts to eat. He loves flapjacks and apple pie and there are ample amounts of both. Jon doesn't respond to the doctor.

"Tell me, Jon, what do you think happened at The End?" asks the doctor.

Jon flinches for just a second. It's illegal to talk about The End because of the emotionally unstable reaction it can cause in certain survivors. It figures the government would ignore its own law.

"We were invaded by the shadow army, a group of supernatural monsters that disappeared shortly after the attack. There were also several bombings, a nerve gas attack, some kind of chemical warfare strike against the civilian population and that all pretty much killed the entire human race," says Jon.

"Really? Is that really what you think happened?" asks the doctor. Jon shrugs again and takes a bite of his food. He chews it slowly. The doctor reaches down behind him and takes out a paper folder.

"Read those," says the doctor. Jon puts down his knife and fork and picks up the folder. It's a collection of random pieces of paper. The first is an official looking military report with the word "classified" stamped across the front.

29/11

Flight patrol commenced at 16:00 hours and lasted 9 hours with pilots Patterson and Dutch from base Charlie 053. Plane nearly ran out of fuel due to pilots not being able to land safely. Pilot Dutch reports wild black river suddenly rising up out of nowhere and "attacking" civilian population. Reports from Patterson contradict reports from Dutch. Patterson indicates he witnessed packs of roving "dark" animals attacking the civilian population, hence he, without waiting for authorisation from central command, unleashed a full artillery strike on the dark creatures inflicting massive collateral damage on civilian population.

Over the course of several hours, Dutch was able to talk Patterson into landing the plane. Both Dutch and Patterson have been detained indefinitely, pending further investigation into "The End" related global incidents.

Jon puts it down and picks up the next piece of paper, a page from a diary.

29/11

```
Mother is dead. Father is dead. A giant black dragon
appeared out of the sky and breathed fire upon our
village. Father says we have been bad people for
aiding the Americans. Perhaps this is why we were
punished. The black dragon spat death for hour upon
hour. Of our family, only me and Sister survive. We
begin today to walk to the hospital. We are both weak
but I believe we will make it. I hope someone finds
this one day and knows what we went through. The
thought makes me feel hopeful.
```

Jon keeps paging. There are articles and notes and reports and a hundred different accounts of the day humanity died. All mention the shadow army at one point or another but there are bits that don't fit together, that don't make sense.

"I don't…I don't understand," says Jon. The doctor scoops another forkful of food into his mouth.

"I'm going to let you in on a little secret," says the doctor. He chews his food.

"The End, when the shadow army invaded, as we call it here, was the worst day in most people's lives. But what many people don't realise is that they had a choice in what kind of day it was. People projected what the worst possible thing that could happen was onto that day and then, in their minds, it happened. It was, in fact, a mass hallucination."

Jon has stopped chewing and the food has turned to ash in Jon's mouth. Jon was there. Jon saw the shadows, he can remember the hand on his leg, the bright light, the smoke, the chaos, the pain, he smelt the gas. And then he remembers Wilfred, the young boy he'd helped out of the school when it happened. Wilfred thought they were being attacked by wolves.

"It's not possible," says Jon. Jon whispers it. He barely breathes it.

"It's entirely possible, Jon," says the doctor. "I know because I was there at the epicentre, as was your father." He puts down his fork and begins to stare intently at Jon.

"And let me ask you this, Jon. Does that kind of hallucination sound familiar to you? The kind of hallucination that the viewer creates themselves? That they project? It should. It's a gift both you and you father shared. He tapped into the noosphere, the global collective consciousness, just like you tap into people's minds. He did it to the entire human race, but as is always the case with your and your father's talent, it was different, for different people. People found their own horror," says the doctor.

"Your father ended the world as you know it, Jon."

Jon's mind is swimming.

"Let me elaborate. You know the shadow army, the invading force that destroyed everything? That was us. It was always us. Half the human race looked like shadows to the other half and we killed each other. We were fighting, killing ourselves. We were our own enemy and officially, we've never discovered where the shadow army went after the attack because, well, they never went anywhere. We were them all along."

"Then what about the war afterwards? Who the hell was I bombing? Who the hell have we been at war with for the past ten years?"

"Ourselves. Always ourselves. It's a tragedy but there's only so many people left in the world capable of farming, of being doctors, of leading, of being of actual use to society and there were too many refugees to take care of."

"So you had us kill each other?"

The doctor sighed and took off his glasses before continuing.

"History is a series of difficult choices. The only reason there's anything left of the human race, the only reason we're still here is because men like me made those difficult choices."

Jon starts to laugh and he does not know where the laughter comes from.

"Look around you, old man. Does it look like we're 'still here' to you?"

"We needed to do what was done. We needed to unite the world and do away with the tribalism and infighting and horror that's been the hallmark of mankind for the last five thousand years." The doctor rubbed his temple, then carried on. "The plan was, there would be a brief attack by an unknown force, the entire global consciousness would fall into a state of despair, a state hopelessness, then it would be followed by a sense of purpose, a sense unification, a sense that the human race could do anything if it stuck together. Your father died in the process. It was too much for him and the machine we used killed him before he could create the sense of purpose in the noosphere. The sense of hope. A destiny, for all mankind. Hence, the world is in a global state of depression and why we must keep feeding the population anti-depressants in the water supply. Otherwise, there's every chance that the world would, within a day or two, kill itself."

"I honestly can't believe that you're trying to justify this slaughter, that you've convinced yourself that what you did, what you are doing, was the right thing. Mankind would've gotten there eventually."

"Eventually? Can you imagine what aliens from another planet would say if they saw us back then? Step out of your narrow mind for a second and see just how horrible we were as a species: people separated by bits of cloth stuck to sticks with the colours of their country sewn onto them, by national anthems, fighting over patches of dirt that we could only lay claim to because we flopped out of our mothers onto them."

Jon fell silent.

"Do you know how much we managed to do because of The End, even considering we failed to finish the project? We invented teleportation in a matter of months. That technology wasn't predicted to become a reality for another hundred years. People had a common threat Jon, even if they didn't know what it was or how it worked. They had something to fear, and scientists and doctors like me, we were finally able to do what we needed to do for the sake of science. Do you have any idea how much modern medicine owes to the Nazis? There are times when the weight of morality is lighter than the weight of survival," says the doctor.

"You're an insane coward. People live in a hell of your design and to stop them from finding out what's really going on, people have technology rations and a disabled Internet," says Jon. "You control what's left of the undernet with an iron fist so people can't talk to each other. And you made it illegal to talk about The End and you've kept everything so vague and everyone so drugged up that even when people do find out, they're not believed," says Jon.

"Do you think we could trust what's left of mankind with the truth? Really, Jon?"

Jon can't believe it. Jon doesn't want to believe it. But something is hardening inside him because all of this feels like truth. The doctor throws a picture in front of Jon; it's the doctor and his father, arm in arm, in front of a giant machine. Smiling.

"My father ended the world," whispers Jon.

"He only ended a bad world, Jon. In the greater scheme of history, it was a small price to pay for all we've managed to accomplish. And in ten days' time, on the ten year anniversary of The End, we're going to accomplish even more," says the doctor. He folds his hands and looks at Jon like a piece on a chessboard.

"What do you mean?"

"I mean we're going to have another cataclysm and you're going to cause it. But we're going to do it right this time, not like the one your father ruined. Your father wasn't completely in control of his powers but we know so much more these days, Jon. We can take your parlour tricks that you've been turning and give you real power. We can help shape the world into a truly better place. Unfortunately, because your father died during the process, we couldn't create new, better ideas within the noosphere. Of uniting society, of coming together as one whole, for the greater good of mankind." The doctor shakes his fist. "Instead, we just had that one final illusion. Catastrophe. Terror. Depression. An apocalypse. Your father's parting gift to the world. The one he died making. Don't you want to make up for it, Jon? Don't you want to fix the world?" asks the doctor.

Jon's brain ticks over the things he's being told like a machine. He feels like he's outside his body, watching someone else do his talking for him.

"You're saying you could amplify my illusions like you did his, and I can create new ones?" asks Jon.

"Not just new, Jon, better. Better for all of us. You were meant for this, born for this, even. I know life has not been fair to you but sometimes, we are nothing more than a ball thrown by a child. You can no more change direction or slow down life than the ball can."

"You are both right and wrong."

"How so?"

"We cannot slow down time. But we can always change direction."

The doctor laughs, stands up and puts his hand on Jon's shoulder.

He leans down, puts his mouth near Jon's ear and says, "Think about it," then walks off.

The guards lead Jon, numb and ice cold, back to the cell. His father killed the world. His father killed an entire planet. His father was responsible. Maybe Jon will be responsible for completely destroying it.

Or saving it.

One night passes.

CHAPTER 12

THE END

A completely undiscovered tribe in Brazil kills themselves, leaving nothing but artifacts for possible future generations to find. Each member of the tribe hugged and kissed every other member of the tribe, then went down to the river and lay down with their feet pointing towards where the sun rose each morning.

A wave of fear, despair, and anguish breaks over the assembled children in Jon's school hall and in every person in every city in the world at once. The pain hits. People drop to their knees in agony. The greatest pain they've ever known. And all they want is not pain. Not pain. Not pain. Not a car, not a winning lottery ticket, not even love. Just not pain. The lucky pass out. When Jon is finally conscious of what's going on around him, when he's no longer blindly running in fear, he finds himself wandering the school in a daze. Children cry. Teachers cry. People flee in all directions at once, monsters are real. Monsters are here. A small child grabs Jon's hand.

"Excuse me, sir, I need to call my mom. I think I need to go home. Please help me call my mom, she'd be worried about the...the wolves," says the child. His eyes are wild. Around them, the shadow creatures leap out of corners and travel in packs, tearing people apart and howling and screaming like animals. The child is delirious. Jon knows what it's like to be afraid. Jon takes his hand and pulls him through the school in no particular direction.

"What's your name?"

"Wilfred, sir."

"No, don't call me sir. We only call grown-ups sir."

"Ok."

"My name is Jon. Wilfred, we're going to get out of here, ok?"

"Ok."

"Do you know what you call a fish with no eyes, Wilfred?"

"No."

"A fshhhh."

The screams of the shadows and a mist made of white light hang over everything and they are the strangest possible accompaniments to Wilfred's giggling. Jon takes Wilfred and pushes through it all, knowing that Wilfred's mind has been taken off everything a little; knowing that it's still possible to tell jokes gives Jon the faintest sense of hope. Jon pushes through.

They make it to the entrance near the carpark where the parents drop their children off each morning. Cars lay on top of cars. Smoke fills the air. Ashes fall. The screams go on and on and on. Jon is more scared than he's ever been. He was the most scared he'd ever been last night. But this is everyone. Everyone is dead or dying. The clock tower has been knocked down. Bricks lie scattered across the playground. In the face of all this, Wilfred sobs hot tears. There is no joke Jon can tell to take his mind off this carnage.

"The wolves…the wolves are eating everyone," says the child.

A lady runs past, blood streaming down her face, chased by shadows. An old man convulses in the street. Chaos lives here now. Chaos and death. Jon starts running towards his home, holding Wilfred's hand, dashing out of the parking lot. They make it to the bushes along the side of the school and Jon sees a pack of shadows rounding a corner, approaching them but before the shadows can see them, he pulls Wilfred and himself into the bushes. Wilfred is still crying and he clamps his hand over Wilfred's mouth until nothing can be heard but muffled sobs. The shadows stop just outside and one takes a step towards where they are, sniffing the air. Jon wills every part of him to be still and wishes to high heaven that Wilfred understands that he needs to be quiet. Suddenly, a house across the road erupts in chaos and broken windows and screams and the pack of shadows leaps towards it as one.

Jon stays still for another few seconds and then leans down to whisper into Wilfred's ear.

"Wilfred, what is green and brown, has six legs and if it fell out of a tree would kill you?"

Wilfred shakes his head.

"A pool table."

Wilfred smiles for a moment and that's enough for Jon. He knows Wilfred won't give up and just start crying on the ground. He jumps out of the bushes, still holding Wilfred's hand and they run as fast as they have ever run in their lives. They make it to Jon's house and Jon fumbles with the key he found in his box of cigarettes that morning and manages to open the door, shoving Wilfred and himself inside before slamming the door shut again. He holds it closed with his body, expecting at any moment for something to slam against it, demanding entry, demanding that they die, screaming.

Jon can hear the sound of the TV in the house and he takes Wilfred with him towards the sound. It sounds strange to have something as normal as a TV on inside this nightmare. He walks into the lounge and Jon's mother is watching the news. Her eyes dart backwards and forwards from them to the TV, not even really registering that they're there. Her normally perfect blonde hair is everywhere at once. She's scratched her forearms bloody. Jon goes to the kitchen and gives Wilfred some milk.

"Stay away from the windows!" Jon's mother hisses at them. Jon nods. Jon is brave for Wilfred and doesn't react, doesn't cry. The newscaster is speaking. The newscaster is out of breath. A ticker tape at the bottom of the screen flashes statistics and details and numbers and short, sharp sentences.

```
...No one has claimed responsibility. An invading army
of shadows has entered every country in the world.
Mass bombings have left billions dead, more injured.
World leaders in emergency meeting...
```

Jon doesn't understand what's happened. His mother is beside him, holding his hand so tightly it hurts. She is crying and blood is dripping down her arm. Now Jon is crying because she is crying. He tries not to let Wilfred see.

"Where's Dad?" asks Jon.

"Your father…I haven't heard from your father."

"He'll be home from work soon," says Jon, his voice breaking slightly. Jon believes this to be true. It is not.

Jon will never see his father again.

There's a knock at the front door. Surely no monster would knock. Jon goes to answer it. Michelle is standing there. Beautiful, sudden love of his life, Michelle. She hugs Jon. And for some reason, Jon believes that despite everything, this is perhaps the only perfect moment the world has ever known, just because she's here and in his arms. Jon knows that whatever cars are still running in the world, all their indicators flicked, at exactly the same moment, perfectly in time, just this once. He knows that two snowflakes are falling somewhere that look exactly the same. He knows that somewhere, people are alive. He forgets about his father for a moment and she consumes his thoughts and it is an escape.

Her body is warm and solid next to his and he holds her tightly and breathes her in.

"Thank God, Jon, thank God you're here. My parents, Jon, my parents were in it and Emily and her parents haven't come back since it happened," she says through a veil of tears. "I was at Emily's house alone watching the TV when the news reports started and…"

"It's ok, it's all going to be ok," Jon says. He thinks this is the right thing to say. He holds her even tighter. She's even more beautiful than he remembers. She cries into his shoulder. His mother cries in the next room. The newscaster is crying. Wilfred is crying. The world is crying. The entire world is in tears. It starts to rain.

The howls of widows and orphans fill the ash-soaked streets. Mushroom clouds appear on the horizon.

Everything is going to be ok.

73

CHAPTER 13

NOW

Somewhere in the last city on Earth, a street child gives his last piece of bread to his hungry younger brother. He writes his name on a wall in chalk, just in case someone will see it and say it aloud one more time. He dies in his sleep that night. His name was Simon. Now you know and Simon will live forever in electrical charges in your brain. You may forget Simon, but never completely. Simon is pure energy in the minds of everyone who reads this, forever.

Inside the United Government compound, a breathless guard is battling to open a cell door, struggling with the keys. The white industrial door isn't budging but he can see inside through a small window.

"He's hung himself!" yells Deformed. Jon's face is bloated and blue and bare of signs of life.

His death mask is beautiful: an evident calm that may have escaped him most of his life. The guards finally manage to open the door. One of them picks up the dead weight of Jon's body and grunts as he lifts it off the hook in the ceiling and ever-so-gently, like a baby, he lays the corpse on the ground.

"The doctor's going to fucking kill us," says the smaller guard.

"Shut up and help me get this noose off his neck," says Deformed.

"Why's it so tight?" asks the quieter one.

"Just fucking cut it. He's probably ripped some of the cabling from the wall and used that," says Deformed. They take out heavy-duty bolt cutters and work on the cables around Jon's neck. They groan with the effort and it takes both of their combined strength to do it but eventually, with a satisfying snap, the noose falls away.

And they are left looking into the eyes of an angry, brown-eyed, half-man, half-tree.

"Who's a coffee table now, numb nuts?" asks Edward as he slams his good arm into Deformed's face, crushing his skull in the process. The smaller guard tries to back away but Edward is on him in an instant, sharp splinters of wood in his hand and ripping apart the frail human body; the smaller, quieter guard is quiet forever. Jon appears from under the covers of one of the bunks.

"How the hell did you manage to make them think I was you?" asks Edward, breathless and covered in blood.

"Easy. It's the ability, the gift I told you about. I just imagined killing myself where you were standing. They thought I'd hung myself, and then removed your collar for you, thinking it was a noose around my neck," says Jon, picking up Deformed's gun from his remains. He's more than a little taken aback by the sheer brutality of Edward's attack. Blood drips from his leaves.

"You're quite a vicious guy, Edward," says Jon, surveying the carnage.

"We need to get going, there's bound to be more of them," says Edward, ignoring whatever Jon just said. As if on cue, an alarm begins to sound, no doubt triggered by the lack of a pulse in the two now very dead guards lying in front of them.

"Come on!" roars Edward, yanking Jon forward out of the cell and into the filthy white industrial corridors. They have no way of knowing where to go or how to get out but both feel that this uncertainty is better than whatever's going to happen to them back in that cell. Jon can hear the doctor's voice down one of the corridors marching, with friends, towards them at speed.

Jon stays put.

"Come on," says Edward and Jon doesn't move.

"Maybe it'd be better if I stayed."

"You're a moron."

"Fair enough."

Jon has a brief moment where he really and truly considers staying there, of going along with everything because fuck it, maybe the world is a better place with a delusion of happiness. It's at least better than a delusion of sadness. The thought quickly fades when he remembers how he, how the world got here. Edward grabs Jon's arm and pulls him forward.

They quicken their pace away from the voice, further into the building until shadows from a second patrol pass along the wall in front of them; Jon and Edward turn quickly, finding a locked cell door. Jon shoots the lock out using Deformed's gun, hoping against hope that the cell will hide them until the search party passes. They spill into the cell and slam the door behind them. Jon drops the gun and it falls to the floor, where a man wrapped in a single piece of dark fabric from head to toe picks it up and looks at it like he's never seen one before in his life. An eye patch covers one eye. He says nothing. Jon and Edward say nothing. All three of them are just staring at each other and at least two of them are breathing heavily.

"He's a silencer," says Edward.

"I thought those were only myths," says Jon.

"I was a myth once," says Edward. Jon looks at him. The silencer looks at him. He reminds Jon of one of the characters from *The Black Kracken* comic books he used to read as a kid. The silencer raises the gun and takes aim at Jon's face.

"No," says Jon, right before the trigger is pulled. The bullet flies past Jon's face, into the head of the guard opening the door behind them. The silencer puts the gun into his belt and calmly walks over the body of the dead guard. Jon and Edward look at each other and shrug as they follow the man in black down the corridor.

"Maybe he knows a way out," says Edward.

"Even if he doesn't, I think things will go better from our perspective, with him involved," says Jon.

They round the corner and walk straight into the mess hall, filled with armed guards, who have been forced to abandon their lunch because of the alarm. Jon isn't sure because his face is covered in black cloth but he senses, something about his eye maybe, that the man in black is smiling. Jon has no idea what the guards did to him but he's glad he's not a guard. Jon decides that the man in black's name is One Eye because if the myths are true about silencers, he knows he'll never get his real name out of him anyway.

The next few seconds unfold slowly, as if everything is happening under water. The man in black walks past a guard dishing up pasta salad and without looking, One Eye reaches out one arm to snap the guard's neck and his other takes the now dead guard's weapon. He now has two guns and he makes them dance in his hands backwards and forwards across the room. Shot after shot finds its home on a uniform some- where in the mess hall; guards dive for cover under tables as Edward roars and lunges forward, his massive body slamming through chairs and counters like they were made of balsa wood. Jon imagines there are more of them than there actually are and he aims the illusion at half of the guards, who begin to desperately kill each other in a fight for survival. Edward is hit in the good arm by a stray bullet but it's a clean shot and goes all the way through; it barely even slows him down. But it does piss him off. One Eye is cornered by fire from three of the guards shooting from behind the counter. He leaps toward them and spins through the air, shooting as he falls to the ground, hitting two guards with one bullet as he lands and stabbing the third guard with a blade that appears from somewhere in his black clothing. Only two guards remain and they're busy desperately trying to strangle each other.

"Are you doing that?" asks Edward.

"Yes," says Jon. One Eye turns to him and his remaining eye goes wide.

"It's pretty impressive," says Edward to One Eye.

"I usually just use it for magic tricks," says Jon.

"Tell me, Jon, and I know we've only just met each other, relatively speaking," says Edward, amongst the carnage in the mess hall.

"Yes?" asks Jon.

"Are you a clever person?" asks Edward.

"I believe I am as clever as you are a tree," says Jon. He's doing his best to not be offended by Edward's gruff manner. He also feels that it is best not to be offended while fighting for one's life.

"So why can't we just use your illusion magic-gifty-thingy to walk out of here and make everyone think we're guards?" asks Edward.

"I've never tried anything like that," says Jon, "but it's worth a shot."

At that moment, guards burst open the doors, guns trained on them, fingers on triggers. No one moves but the three of them tense, ready to fight.

"Which way did they go?" yells the commander at the front. Edward raises his limp wooden arm towards the door they came through.

"Right, you lot get to the ER and get patched up, the rest of you, with me," says the guard in charge. They storm past the three of them, not paying them any heed.

"I'm glad you're here with me, Edward, you're quite clever," says Jon.

"I'm glad I'm here with you, too, Jon," says Edward. One Eye sighs and starts walking. They follow him out into another long white corridor, the red emergency lights still flashing but the sirens are suddenly silenced.

"I guess everyone who needs know that we've escaped, knows," says Edward.

"I guess so," says Jon. They find an elevator, One Eye fiddles with wires in the control panel and after the doors slide open seconds later, they jump inside. The elevator starts to go down. Jon doesn't turn to face the glass wall to the outside world, in case there's an army parked outside waiting for them. He doesn't want to know.

"Next stop, basement parking," says an electronic voice.

The three of them breathe heavily from exhaustion and stress, as if they're trying to breathe as much air as they can before they die. The elevator music plays just for them. The doors slide open and the basement appears barren, save for one Peace Carriage and a guard busy polishing it. He turns to them.

"Do you lot know what's going on upstairs?" asks the guard.

"Yes," says Edward. "We've escaped." He picks up the guard by the foot and hurls him across the parking bays and he hits the opposite wall with a sickening wet crunch. They get inside the Peace Carriage. One Eye opens a panel on the interior wall and fiddles with the wires. Nothing.

"Come on!" yells Edward and One Eye scowls at him, still fiddling. Edward pushes him out the way and starts punching one of the control panels. The mechanical horse at the front of the carriage comes to life and they jerk forward, galloping hard towards the giant garage doors.

"What about the door?" says Jon. One Eye looks at him.

"He says 'Fuck the door,'" says Edward.

One Eye pushes some more buttons in what remains of the control panel and the rather impressive arsenal at the disposal of the Peace

Ambassadors makes itself known. A plume of fire launches from the mouth of the mechanical horse and the door melts away before them. Metal drips around them as they burst through, bullets from sentry guns outside bouncing off the hardened shields of the Peace Carriage. And then they're through, into the deserted streets below the United Government compound.

"I know you can hear me, Jon," says the doctor.

CHAPTER 14

NOW

A team of scientists in white lab coats and Peace Ambassadors in full body armour knock down the door of an abandoned apartment, somewhere on the poor side of NewLand, which is most sides. There, they find the resting, almost tranquil dead bodies of a family. One woman, two young children. She killed herself and them; a bottle of brake fluid lies empty nearby. She kept track of every day leading up to it in her diary. One of the scientists picks it up and pages through it, considers it for a moment and then puts it in a clear plastic bag.
"Can we use it?"
"Yes we can."
"Look for more."

Racing away from the United Government building in the stolen Peace Carriage, Jon looks around wildly, trying to find the source of the doctor's voice. There's a screen mounted on one of the panels inside the carriage and the doctor's face leers out of it. Jon wonders if he reached out, punched the doctor in the face, would he feel it? One Eye picks up a keyboard and begins to type furiously.

'Don't respond. He's broadcasting to every screen in every Peace Carriage and in every room in the building. If you respond, he'll know exactly where you are.'

Jon reads what One Eye's written and then nods.

"Where are you going, Jon? Home to Michelle? To your ghost?" the doctor's voice challenges him.

"Who's Michelle?" asks Edward.

Jon ignores him and stares intently at the screen, straight into the doctor's eyes.

"You do know you're living with a ghost, don't you, Jon? My men had trouble figuring it out but once I'd gone over the video footage and other surveillance material we've been gathering on you for the past few years, I worked it out. I worked out why she kept disappearing when you weren't looking. It's because you make her, Jon. It's because she's only in your head. It must be nice living with a dream girl, Jon. A perfect girl. A girl who accepts you no matter what. Who never expects you to change. So romantic. Don't believe me? Ask yourself, when was the last time you had a fight with Michelle you didn't win? Does that sound normal to you, Jon? The girl you love is one of your own illusions. And she's such a good illusion, she even fooled you—" The doctor's voice is starting to get garbled as city feeds interrupt the broadcast.

It takes Jon time but each word from the doctor slowly filters through. He knows that the doctor might kill billions, but he doesn't lie. Jon thinks back to every memory he has of Michelle and for the first time, he starts to consider how she always sleeps if he has nothing to say to her, how she's always awake when he does. How she fades away into the periphery when he goes to Emily's or the Cabaret.

"We need to go back to my apartment," says Jon.

"That's the first place they'll look for you," says Edward.

"I don't care. I need to go home to Michelle."

Just then, the screen flickers back on, picking up a signal again and on the screen is a low-res video of Jon walking around his apartment while Michelle sleeps. The doctor's obviously sending this, messing with his head. He gets into bed and after a few seconds, he's asleep and slowly, Michelle fades away. She just disappears from the video.

The truth slowly settles on Jon's heart like an anchor.

And his heart dies. And every fibre of his being suddenly seems to be screaming for him to hang himself, like the illusion in the cell.

"No," whispers Jon. He reaches for the transmit button on the panel, to yell at the doctor, to confront him, to tell him that Michelle is real. One Eye smacks his hand away. Jon struggles and One Eye grabs him and holds him in a choke hold to stop him from giving them away. Deep down, Jon knows that the love of his life is a figment of his imagination. A ten-year-long dream.

"What the hell is this? What's he talking about? What dream girl?" asks Edward as One Eye restrains Jon.

"She's all I fucking have," says Jon through One Eye's choke hold. Jon's heart finds some kindness; it overrules his brain and makes him pass out. The last thing he hears is the doctor's garbled voice slowly rising to a scream.

"I will find you, Jon! I will find you! I'm coming fo—"

CHAPTER 15

NOW

Inside a Massively Multiplayer Online role playing
game, ten years ago.

<RiftBlood> What time are we supposed to be raiding?

<Ganther> Around 10 pm local time, here in New York,
not sure what time it'll be for you in the UK.

<RiftBlood> I'll work it out. Everything cool?

<Ganther> Yip but I think there's some kind of bug,
the entire New Zealand clan, then all of the Ozzies
and a whole bunch of the Russians just dropped off the
server one after another.

<RiftBlood> That's weird.

<Ganther> Yeah, I've never heard of a bug that rolls
across the planet, usually everyone drops off the
server at once or everything's fine.

<RiftBlood> The admins are usually quite good with
this sort of thing, they'll sort it out quickly.

<Ganther> Yeah. Fuck, Sweden just went. WTF?

<RiftBlood> That's so fucking strange. Hold on,
there's a knock at the door, I'll be right back.

5 minutes ago.

10 minutes ago.

<Ganther> Dude, are you still there?

<Ganther> I'm going to cancel tonight. There's no way
we can get organised if the server's going to fuck-
out every five seconds, none of the other clans have
come back online. I'm going to take some screenshots
of what happened so I can send them to the admins

```
tomorrow. Haha, now there's a knock at my door.
Freaky. Will catch you tomorrow.
<server disconnected>
```

Ten years later, Jon stays unconscious and dreams as Edward and One Eye swerve the stolen Peace Carriage through the streets, outrunning the collected forces of the United Government. In his dream, Jon's driving a convertible. The sun is beautiful and warm on his skin. He doesn't know why, but he's going to a wedding. He pulls up and parks just off the dirt road outside a hotel; a few metres away, the sea rushes the land against some nearby cliffs, again and again. He goes inside.

"Name, sir?"

"Jon Salt."

The words feel so strange. The powdered wig on the concierge bobs from left to right over the guest list as he scans for the name of the lithe young man in front of him before nodding and waving him in with his tablet.

Inside, four young ladies play invisible violins, their hands hovering in the air where the strings once were on these mongrel children of Theramins and synthesizers. He looks down at the wedding invitation in his hand. The date reads 21/11. That's the date The End happened, still eight days away. Or nearly ten years ago.

Jon suddenly feels sick. Edward swerves the Peace Carriage around a particular tricky corner.

Jon sees Emily again, for what feels like the first time that day, at her brother's wedding. He's been told they'll be having it at a Renaissance Halo Hotel and he doesn't expect much out of the event. If Halo Hotels, hotels set in different holographic realities, still exist, then this is after The End but why is everything so different, Jon asks himself, under his breath, trying to win a fight against a dream. Where are the starving children? Where's the decay? Where's the darkness?

He does his best to hold on to where he is and to remember what the score is, what's happened, what hasn't happened yet.

Emily isn't a drug dealer yet. She's just a girl. No. A young adult. But their lives were never like this. Never normal.

And when he really looks at her, her face hits him with all the speed of thought and memory. Even across the room, he can see her pupils dilate as they meet his.

Forgoing any pretenses, he makes his way through the crowd, trying to not make eye contact with anyone in case they remember him and try to draw him into a conversation, a conversation he's had a thousand times before, for all he knows. Now he's afraid he's in a loop, one of the ghosts doing the same thing over and over again, never remembering that he's done it all before. He doesn't know why he remembers and no one else does. No that wasn't true; sometimes they remember but only for a moment, then back to wherever, however they were supposed to be. What scares him more than anything is the idea that he also forgets. Maybe he just didn't, couldn't know when that happened. He'd been told once that you were a new person every time you woke up. Maybe he just thinks he remembers. Fear tiptoed through his mind.

Please let this be the first time I say these things, please let this not be a loop, he begs himself.

"Hello, Emily," says Jon.

"Jon. It's Jon, right?" asks Emily.

Everything seems so normal here. She doesn't remember him yet once, she trusted him enough to show him a mole on her thigh that she thought was ugly. It was just a few centimetres above her garter belt right now.

He thinks of what it would be like to kiss her and the image warms his blood and makes his chest rise. He figures that surely everyone must do that: imagine what it must be like to kiss her. He wonders if they have fantasies of rescuing her if something happens, a mugging, terrorism, something. And then they would kiss, naturally.

Maybe when you stop doing drugs, you forget everything that happened while you were on them. Maybe you made yourself forget, you blocked it out. He thought she was beautiful then, in her disheveled way in the city of NewLand, in the dark present that felt so distant and she was beautiful now, here at this wedding but in a much more elegant, acceptable way. Her uncombed hair, combed. More people than just him would've thought she was beautiful now.

"You really don't remember me?" asks Jon.

"No. Vaguely, maybe…I know your name and I know why we know each other but I don't remember the specifics of it all. That was then.

You know that. It's all…kind of…" says Emily, gesturing halfheartedly.

"I know that," says Jon.

She'd stopped. He'd stopped. Were they normal here? Is this what could have been? Drugs, like misery, require company. Even if your only company is the drug itself. It is always something. You can't talk about the mysteries of the universe and the secret joy to be found within each object in it to yourself all night. Or maybe you can.

Jon knows that something is wrong with Michelle. Her name is like an itch inside his head he can't scratch. But here, in this dream, he cannot make sense of any of it. He remembers a man who was half-tree and half-man and a man dressed in black with one eye and a man who said he knew his father. An evil man. But now he's here. With Emily. She'd always been his sounding board and he had been hers. When he saw rain falling up from the ground, she saw it too. When she saw spiders, he saw them too and he batted them away from her and made her feel safe. Although, admittedly some of those visions were his fault. She thought it was just the drugs at first but she'd worked out that some of it, some of it was him. Here, she's an accountant. She probably isn't but she says something corporate when he asks her what she does for a living now. Everything's so beautifully boring.

"I wanted to want you like you wanted me to. But I couldn't," says Jon.

"What?" asks Emily.

"Nothing."

"You were friends with some of my friends, I know that." It was a question disguised as a statement. She really doesn't remember much. She's been treated to forget, that's what he couldn't put his finger on. That's why things were so strange. Things moved so slowly here. Her parents had taken her for a memory wipe, that was it. Or maybe they were just stuck somewhere else and couldn't go back to who they once were. Everything moved like it was covered in syrup.

"We grew up in the same neighbourhood," says Jon.

"I know that, you don't have to explain," says Emily.

"Do you remember the night on the swings when I first met Michelle?"

She answers his question with a blank stare and half a sound that says she doesn't.

Her red hair continues to fall.

"You're the one who said you didn't remember me."

"It's not like I'm ashamed of those days but, they were something maybe everyone goes through, you know? You mess around, have fun but one day, we all have to grow up. When did you stop using?"

"Oh, shortly after I moved away," says Jon. And he's telling the truth. Everything is normal. Life is normal here. Everything else was a dream.

The conversation's going to become awkward and stilted soon, he remembers that. He's been here before. This is a loop. He's sure of it now. He starts to sweat a little. That makes no sense. There's no reason for him to think he's in a loop but the fear is there. How many times have I driven up to this hotel? How many times?

"Do you remember Michelle at least?" asks Jon.

"Michelle? I had a friend in high school called Michelle but I can't remember ever introducing the two of you," says Emily.

He sighs.

All the people he knew, all the people he'd ever met were trapped in the past. Now, on this day, in this place, only these new people existed. With jobs and houses and kids either already here or on the way. And Emily, who used to be his best friend, is further away than anyone.

Emily sees someone else she hasn't seen for a long time and waves at them, then mumbles something that people mumble when they're going to leave for a while, something about seeing you later, lovely chatting to you, that sort of thing. Sometimes he doesn't remember what people say, just what people mean. I need this. I don't want that. Do this for me. I appreciate you. I hate you. I love you. Just the meaning, not the specifics. God had never once lived or loved in these details.

She turns and leaves and as she does, the light from the sea catches her red hair and turns it into a veil of light, some kind of burning halo, just for a second and then it's gone again. He turns and looks out at the sea as the sun sluggishly works its way across the water. Everything shimmers in the orange haze of late afternoon. The light hurts his eyes and he's forgotten his sunglasses in the car; quickly, he's blinking away tears. He's got a car here. There are no trains. No Peace Carriages. No doctors.

"I've never known you to be so emotional at a wedding, Jon," says James, Gentle James, another person he once knew but now didn't.

They'd been friends at school hadn't they? James swishes a bottle of scotch and hangs onto him. He used to knock on Jon's window at night and they'd go out and smash letterboxes and run riot through the streets. No. No, they'd flown planes together and they'd bombed people, people he'd been told were the enemy. But that doesn't make sense. Jon's never flown a plane in his life. He went to design school.

"You know me, James, always the crybaby." He jokes in the way people from years ago did, like they once were. It's the harshness of friends you haven't seen for a while and who knew you once used to mean, "I love you" when you said, "hello."

He hates weddings. On behalf of the bride and groom and on his own accord as well. Weddings are about everyone else except the bride and groom. They are an excuse for families to get together and see each other and compare notes about what life is and where it's supposed to be taking them.

"What are you doing these days?" asks James. They both slipped into the same trance.

"I'm a graphic designer," says Jon.

"Really? How long have you been doing that for?" says James, Gentle James and Jon wants to say I threw your dead body out of a plane and it burst into flames and I cried so hard for so long and they took all my memories and I miss you, I miss you so much. But instead, he says, "Too long."

"Where do you work?" asks James.

"Carnal, The Neon Jump-Rope, Bigsy's," says Jon, listing them off like great battles. I miss you my friend, I miss you.

"Never heard of any of those," says James.

"Obviously," says Jon. "And yourself? Still trying to crack a career as a professional clown?"

"That's just a side gig now, now I'm an accountant," says James.

"Awesome, that sounds like fun. What exactly does that entail?" asks Jon with just a hint of sarcasm.

His mind immediately starts kicking around its bedroom, going through boxes and shelves and old books because it knows it won't be needed for at least the next forty-five to sixty seconds while someone tells him something he really doesn't care about. James never died. He's still here. They never bombed anyone. Jon never had his tattoos cut off in a camp. In the boxes Jon's kicking around in his head, there's an eye-patch and a branch and a stethoscope. Jon doesn't know why. Things move slowly.

Mumble, sharp word, soft word, swearing, next sentence, sharp word, sharp word, soft word, gesturing, the tone of someone who really believes what they're telling you is a paradigm shift in their respective industry. Question. Pause.

Shit.

"I'm sorry, what was that last bit?" asks Jon.

"I asked you if you were really listening to me and you just nodded your head," says James.

He isn't actually kidding or being mean to be funny, he's genuinely offended. Sweet, Gentle James staggers, just a little, his body fighting gravity and the booze.

"I'm sorry James, I really didn't mean to but I just remembered I've got work to finish for tomorrow and I got distracted," says Jon.

"Whatever, haha," he snakes drunkenly back into the core of the wedding, looking for one more familiar face.

You do get to make a second impression, as long as it's nearly ten years later, in a place like this, and this was a terrible one. It really does upset him but more in the way that he knows he should be upset about it and should use that bad feeling as a way to motivate himself to be a better person, but it doesn't. He's upset because he just can't get upset about things that should matter anymore.

He has just one more drink, says goodbye to the married couple and then leaves. Early day tomorrow, big presentations in the afternoon. He walks across the parking lot, opens the door to his car, the convertible he's always wanted, and gets in. He takes the top down before he gets out of the parking lot as he figures the wind will keep him awake. He feels like he's just watched the people he once knew drown and die in the people they thought they'd wanted to be.

Something bad has happened or was going to happen today, somewhere but not here. Phantom memories tease his brain. There was a wooden monster, a man with a white beard, Michelle, Michelle, Michelle. Where's Michelle? And Emily? Why did things feel so wrong? Everything came into view sharply and then disappeared just as quickly.

The sun explodes overhead in a thin white line, hot on his face as it turns the coastline into cascading lava pits. The creatures of the sea kill themselves on the white sand while tanned bodies move like out of focus ghosts, on their way to the other side of the sun. It's happening again, Jon tells himself as the blast wave devastates the surrounding countryside and a wave of shadows howling and calling for blood crash over the remains. I did this. I do this. I will do this.

Suddenly he's not there; he finds himself next to Michelle on a couch and there's another power failure. He's telling her how much he loves her and she's smiling and nodding. He kisses the back of her neck and she smiles some more and they make love and he thinks he knows what happiness feels like and some part of him just wants someone else to touch him and tell him he's real. She does that and she asks for so, so little in return.

And now they're walking through a park holding hands and she lets go because she sees a child lying on the ground and he's hungry. She forces Jon to go home and get some food from the MicroPVR and bring it back. He grumbles about it but he loves her for it and he'll never admit it. He hates the world but he loves her because she doesn't.

And now he's drunk and verbose; they're at the Cabaret and they're arguing, fighting.

"You know what the problem is? You buy things and then you keep them clean. You take care of them. Keep them in a special pocket. Away from keys and coins. Away from other things that should be kept clean and taken care of as well. Then they get scratched by accident. And scratched again. And again. And again. And again. Soon, you don't care about them anymore. You don't keep them in a special pocket. You throw them in the bag with everything else. They've surpassed their form and become nothing but function. People are like that. You meet them and keep them clean. In a special pocket. And then you start to scratch them. Not on purpose. Sometimes you just drop them by accident or forget which pocket they're in. But after the first scratch, it's all downhill from there. You see past their form. They become function. They are a use, nothing more," says Jon and even he does not know what he means anymore.

"Are you talking about me?" asks Michelle.

"No. I'm just tired," says Jon.

"I love you."

"Ok."

"...ok," says Michelle.

Now they're somewhere else and Jon finds himself talking at her, not to her, lecturing her because he's so fucking smart.

"You watch the news and think you're informed. You listen to the radio and think you enjoy music. You speak to the same friends you've had since high school and think you're socialites. I know better. I'm better. But thinking that just makes me feel worse," says Jon.

"...You don't have to like me or who I am but I do love you."

"I said ok."

"Bu—" begins Michelle.

"OK."

He gets up and looks for something to slam, something to make his point. She buries her head in her hands and cries. Ok. I'm fine. I'm just tired. The things people say when they don't know why they're fighting anymore and just want to go to bed.

Now he's just talking at the air and she's sleeping. "I wish I knew what a traffic jam felt like. I wish I knew what being afraid of doing your taxes was like. What it felt like to be bored of a job or to really, really hate one, to feel like you were doing what you had to do to survive and not what you wanted to do. I wish I knew what it was like to have kids. I wish I knew what a hot dog that didn't come out of the PVR tasted like. I wish I knew what going on holiday was like. All of that seems so much easier to deal with than this," and he rambles on, until the sun comes up.

Jon's feels like he's outside himself, looking at himself doing this and for the first time in his life, wonders if he's the biggest asshole to ever live or if anything has ever been real or even mattered.

Ok.

I'm just tired.

Fine.

CHAPTER 16

NOW

The man with the white beard puts man after man into the machine, plugs in all the right photographs, screenshots, diaries, artifacts, metaphors, and symbols and all the men scream with so much despair. Each one is a story. Then the men, their noses start to bleed and their voices are filled with pure terror and then they die. And he does it again and again. Into infinity. The words appear on all the TV screens across the planet, "You have read this all before."

Jon wakes up screaming.

"Ok, ok, buddy, relax," says Edward's voice, from somewhere.

Jon's covered in sweat, and more tired than he's ever been in his life. It wasn't a dream. This is real. This is real, he tells himself again and again and the words echo off into a cavern in his mind.

"You got an infection or got poisoned or went insane or something and you've been out for more than a day, yelling some of the craziest shit I've ever heard," says Edward, slowly coming into focus behind a haze. He puts a glass of water to Jon's lip and Jon notices that they feel like they're on fire. Then he notices a large chunk of his wrist is missing.

"Did I get shot?"

"Nope, we had to take out your wrist implant so they couldn't track you. Mine got taken when they took my arm. Our deadly friend did a little minor surgery on you, quite delicately I might add, then he did himself. Bastard didn't even use anesthetic, just ripped it clean out."

"Thank you. And call him One Eye, he's not going to give us his real name," says Jon, rubbing his arm.

"No problem, thanks for saving my life back in the cell and bandaging up my arm. And don't forget to thank One Eye. He did all of the hard work," says Edward.

One Eye looks across at Jon from the other side of the old warehouse and waves. Once. He scares Jon, just a little. He rubs his arm. The wound itches but it feels slightly better.

"We had to get rid of the Peace Carriage. One Eye destroyed whatever was in it that could conceivably track us but we couldn't be absolutely sure. So we trashed the lot of it. Well, almost the lot of it. We kept an undernet interface," says Edward. Jon sees the stripped out interior laying up against the side of the warehouse wall.

"Dad was a mechanic," says Edward. "He showed me how to strip any machine in less than ten minutes. Even one handed." Jon notices the stump where Edward's arm used to be. The stump is getting longer. Some of the myths are true.

"Here, eat this," says Edward.

He gives Jon some protein bars that taste like grilled cheese sandwiches. Jon opens the wrapper and the chemicals in the bars react with the air and they heat up in his hands. They're the most delicious things Jon's ever eaten, or he's so hungry they just taste that way. Jon begins to feel human again. An hour later, he's up and walking around but something in his heart is dead. He remembers what the doctor said about Michelle now. What he saw in the video. Michelle is a ghost. Michelle is a ghost. Michelle is a ghost. No matter how many times he says it, it doesn't feel real. Edward is fiddling with one of the hologram networks that still runs through the undernet, cobbled together from the remains of the carriage. Edward sighs and steps back. He can tell something's eating Jon up inside.

"Jon," says Edward.

"Yes?" asks Jon.

"What was the doctor guy talking about, who's Michelle?"

"It's a long story. Maybe a ghost. Maybe she's a ghost," says Jon. Jon stares off at a distant point that maybe, he once reached. Edward decides that now is the right time to talk about something else.

"I'm afraid we're stuck with each other," says Edward.

"Why?"

"Well, because all three of us have just become the most wanted fucking people on the planet. We killed a whole bunch of them."

"Uh-huh," says Jon. He doesn't seem to care.

"Look at the globe feed coming from the undernet, from the people who spend their rations on it," says Edward, still trying to take Jon's mind away from wherever it is because he can see it's not a nice place.

"What about it?" asks Jon.

"Well, you see all that stuff in the feed? All the stuff that gets up-voted and praised?" asks Edward.

"Yeah," says Jon.

"Other people chose that right?" asks Edward.

"Right," says Jon.

"So right now you're looking at the most popular content, pictures of cats and shit, across what's left of the world right?" asks Edward.

"Right. That's a good thing. People love that, the triviality of what used to be the Internet gives them a sense of comfort," says Jon, not sure what Edward is getting at.

"No it's not," says Edward.

"Popular stuff is bad?" asks Jon.

"No, disregarding your own personal taste in favour of the rest of the world's taste is bad. Sitting there, waiting for something interesting to come over the feed, sent to you and pre-approved by someone else, that's bad. That's why the art director and the copywriter on your block used to call you a consumer. Because that's what you do. You just lie there and consume. Like a fat pupa and they can harvest you when they want to," says Edward.

"You sound upset," says Jon.

"The whole thing's upsetting. Remember all the networks and applications and socialising people were expected to do, when all that shit was still allowed?"

"Are you going to tell me that was bad, too?"

"Too many people mistook envy for happiness. They believed other people wanting to do the things they were doing was more important that doing the things they wanted to do. So they'd edit their photographs and edit their lives and edit and lie until from a distance, it looked like they had the perfect life. But life isn't something that should be edited. Life shouldn't be cut. The only way you'll ever discover what it truly means to be alive and human is by sharing the full experience of what it means to be human and each blemish and freckle that comes with it."

"You're an ent, Edward, not a human. Why should I, or you, care what it means to be human? I don't care where the chemicals in my drugs come from or where the grapes, in what passes for wine these days, were grown."

"Perhaps. Perhaps that's why you drink wine and take drugs. Because you want to kill the question."

"Or I drink wine because my head likes being drunk and I take Sadness so I can actually feel something besides the fucking chemically induced happiness the government puts in the water in this God forsaken city. Not everything is some big philosophical fuck-show."

"I disagree."

"Fine. But life is what you make of it. Plenty of people have lived and died, perfectly content, without ever having asked why the sun rises in the east and sets in the west."

"Jon, if you can show me a life without a question, I'll show you someone without purpose."

"You're starting to sound upset, Edward."

"Of course I'm not upset. I'm not allowed to be, am I," says Edward and he takes a swig from his water bottle.

"I'd give my kingdom to care," says Jon.

"Why the hell are you being so goddamn melodramatic?"

"Why the hell are you trying to be so fucking philosophical? And since when did you give a shit about any of this anyway? I don't even fucking know you."

Jon can see he's hurt Edward somehow, some way. He's not used to having conversations like this. He avoids them. Edward turns away and goes back to the remains of the Peace Carriage. Maybe trying to get Jon's mind off whatever was bothering him was a bad idea. Maybe not. He'd rather have Jon turn his anger outwards than inwards. He cares about the stupid human. It's a strange emotion. He knows Jon saved his life. He's indebted. Each of them owes the other something.

Jon shakes his head and leaves to go back to the makeshift mattress. He's usually had several doses of Sadness by now and the withdrawal's making him a little crazy. And Michelle. Michelle, Michelle, Michelle, whatever she was, wherever she was. He felt like the last ten years hadn't happened. Around him, black plastic trinkets with single red lights and swipe screens, interactive sensors and tangible interfaces, float in the air like neon snowflakes. The future is tacky.

They'll have to work out what to do next; the doctor will be hunting them but there's an unspoken understanding that whatever they do, it can wait until morning. Jon sleeps the rest of the day and that night, they sit around a space heater with all the lights switched off, keeping an eye out for any Peace Patrols.

"You know they used to pay the crime writers more," says Edward, chewing on a protein bar.

"What do you mean?" asks Jon.

"You know when sometimes they show old shows like *CSI* or *Law & Order* on the news blimp? The guys who worked on that stuff made more money," says Edward.

"Why?" asks Jon.

"Because they wanted everyone who got home each night to learn the same lesson each time and that lesson is so important, they used to pay them more," says Edward.

"And what lesson was that?" asks Jon.

"Do the wrong thing and you'll get caught," says Edward.

"We should try not to do that then," says Jon.

"The fucking cops are the only ones who got to live in the future. They're the only ones who got to see what technology could really do. The rest of us get the scraps. The technology rations. But they're still a bunch of morons," says Edward.

"Now I'm confused. Are you telling me I will or I won't get caught if I do bad things?" asks Jon. It's fun to wind Edward up and for a moment, it distracts him from the missing space inside him.

"I'm telling you that everyone in this time, in this place, is playing a lottery with very few winning numbers, whether anyone wants to admit it or not," says Edward.

"Now who's being melodramatic?" asks Jon.

Jon's comment cracks the tension and they laugh and then they notice that One Eye is laughing, too. It is the strangest laugh they've ever heard, like two cans filled with pennies scraping against each other.

Edward and Jon slowly turn to look at him, stopping laughing. One Eye slowly stops. There's a silence.

And then, they begin to laugh again.

CHAPTER 17

NOW

The last man alive in Africa has survived ten years but now he's convinced that the sun is finally going to burn him out. He crawls through the shack he's in and edges up to the windows, careful not to let the sun touch his skin. Each morning, he puts paper over the windows and by the time the sun goes down, they're burnt up. He writes messages on bits of newspaper, should anyone ever find this place again, so they could know what happened. So they could know what he went through. The idea that someone one day might know what happened is the only thing that brings a smile to his parched, cracked lips and he only allows himself to think of it once a day, in case the thought stops bringing him happiness. He rations his own happiness. He leaves the notes under rocks, away from the sun, so they won't get burnt up. Late at night, he thinks he can still hear the shadows outside.

On the other side of the world, One Eye and Edward are asleep. Jon has something he needs to do. Some part of him accepts it and some part of him knows he's just talking to a piece of himself but it's a piece that he once loved. A piece that he still loves.

He thinks of Michelle.

And she's there.

As if she's always been there. A single tear runs down Jon's face.

"Do you know that those cigarettes we smoked in the park, that night we first met, that's the last time I ever smoked," says Jon.

"Of course I know. Why wouldn't I know? I've known you forever, Jon. I know every inch of you," says Michelle.

"I just didn't want to ever smoke another one, because everything changed with that cigarette and I didn't want things to change ever again."

"I know."

"You know because you're just a figment of my imagination, aren't you?"

Michelle nods and bites her lip. "I never meant to hurt you, Jon. I'm a part of you. I didn't want to hurt myself. I didn't want to hurt us. I had to keep the truth hidden."

"How are you so beautiful?" asks Jon and he touches her face.

"What?"

"I said: how are you so beautiful?" repeats Jon.

"I heard you, I just didn't understand the question," says Michelle.

"Do you understand it now that I've said it again?" asks Jon.

"No…not really. I don't have a choice in how I look. I just look how I look. This is how the universe made me," says Michelle.

"But you're not beautiful because of how you look," says Jon.

"Then what makes me beautiful?" asks Michelle.

"Something else I guess," says Jon. He looks at the stars through the holes in the roof and wishes they would rain down on him. He knows now, he knows she's a lie but she's a comforting lie.

"You're the one that thinks I'm beautiful. I don't look in the mirror and think that. It's a quality you give me so if anyone should know 'how' I am beautiful, it should be you," says Michelle.

He thinks about it for a while and then leans forward and kisses her on the forehead.

"I guess that's fair," says Jon. They are quiet with each other for a while, and then Jon carries on, "Why do I hurt the way I hurt?"

"Why would I know that?"

"Because," and Jon hurts so much right now, it hurts so much to say, "Because you're from my head. You can see things in there that I cannot." He is crying so softly. Michelle looks at him and frowns a little. She nods.

"Because the chemicals in your brain come from your father. Because your gift is a curse. Because you have seen too many things. You have heard and read too many words. You have too many ways of describing your hurt. It is not a dull ache. It is a sharp, intricate thing inside you, twisting and turning as it cuts throu—" Jon's startled by a sudden rustling behind him. Edward is awake and next to him.

"Who the hell is that?" Edward asks and immediately, Michelle fades and disappears.

"No one."

"This is kind of fucked up. Is this like a porn thing? You imagine some broad to bang and then she's there?" asks Edward, trying not to laugh.

Before he knows it, Jon is across the room with a pistol he'd taken from the remains of the Peace Carriage cocked and pointed at the heart of Edward's trunk, black flames licking him up and down.

"What the hell?"

"Don't you ever call her that ever again. Ever," says Jon, breathlessly.

"Who? What the hell is going on? Is that Michelle?" asks Edward.

Jon slowly returns to himself and the violence leaves his red eyes.

"I'm sorry, Edward. I'm sorry, I just wasn't expecting you."

"I'm going to ask again, what the hell is going on?"

"I can't tell you," says Jon, turning away from him.

"Why not?" asks Edward, taking Jon by the shoulder and turning him back around.

"Because I can't."

"We're running away from every Peace Ambassador in the last city on Earth, hiding away in an old warehouse and relying on each other to survive and according to what you've told me, the world might be ending, again, in less than a few days and it might be your fault. I think you can tell me," says Edward.

"She's a girl," says Jon.

"I can see that, I'm a tree, not a fucking moron. She's obviously a little more than that," says Edward.

"She's the only girl I ever loved," says Jon.

"The one that got away?" asks Edward.

"Calling her 'the one' implies that there were or have been others. There haven't," says Jon.

"You've only ever loved one woman in your whole life?" asks Edward. His eyes are wide.

"Yes," says Jon.

"That's crazy," says Edward.

"Maybe. It's just me. Maybe I'm crazy," says Jon.

"I know you're crazy. I just didn't know you were that crazy," says Edward.

"She's just the only thing I think of when I think of love," says Jon.

"How long ago was this?" asks Edward.

"What?"

"Her. This. This infatuation. When did it start?" asks Edward.

"When I met her. When I was sixteen," says Jon.

"When you were sixteen?!" exclaims Edward.

"Yes. From The End onwards," says Jon.

"Is she really a ghost?"

"She's a part of me that I don't understand," says Jon.

"And you can't just get over her?"

"She's like a cancer in my mind and some part of me knows that she'll be there until I die. Some part of me knows that she'll kill me. There's nothing I can do that she won't be in. I could drink water and it would taste like her lips. I could stare at the sky and the birds flying by would be there like the first time we kissed. And you know what? None of it was real. Not one moment. She's was my whole life and now I'm left with nothing but the fragment of a broken memory. Less than a moment. I built my heart around her in the time it took to smoke two cigarettes."

"That's a bit fucking much, is it really that bad?"

"She ruined my whole life."

"Were you happy when you were with her?"

"Yes."

"Then she didn't ruin anything. What happens or happened to her doesn't even matter. What happens to you now, that's the important bit."

Jon is quiet for a moment.

"Thank you, Edward, I think."

"For what?"

"For not being the rest of the world. For not being alien," says Jon.

"I think that's the nicest thing anyone's ever said to me," says Edward.

Jon is surprised to find himself friends with a tree and mythological assassin. And soon, he's sleeping in a warehouse with them. But the girl he thought he loved haunts his dreams and doesn't give him any rest.

CHAPTER 18

NOW

The gentleman put in charge of Kurt Cobain's guitars picks one up and starts to play. He plays *Polly*. He knows it's about a girl being raped. His mother was raped. His father was a rapist. He's never told anyone. Now only this guitar knows. He whispers the lyrics to the dark room he finds himself in. Then he starts to cry, wretched, heartfelt sobs that wrack his body.

The doctor's hesitant to lean against the side of the plane, even though he's tired. He knows if he wants to rest his head on the plastic wall next him, others must have wanted to and probably had. There's an ancient civilization's worth of sweat and untraceable but imaginable humanness in that wall. Maybe they disinfected it after every flight. Probably not. They probably just told people they did that. But they really didn't. Lies are cheaper than disinfectant. He doubts they have enough people left to run that tight a ship. He tries to ignore it. This plane is the only way to travel long distances, even for someone as high up as him.

The last plane on Earth flies past a looping crash. Someone had once tried to save a passenger airplane with an emergency teleportation field in front of it, but they'd messed up something and now the plane just teleported 1000 feet from where it was and then crashed again. The people in the cabin had screamed for their lives and held the hands of the ones they loved a million times, never knowing that they were always going to die and that also, they were never going to die.

Everything was just a loop, stretching into infinity.

No matter, thinks the doctor, he's on his way to meet somebody important. Someone Jon loves. Someone the doctor can use. And he smiles.

CHAPTER 19

NOW

"What have you got there?"
"This is the rope that Ian Curtis hung himself with."
"Who's Ian Curtis?"
"He was the lead singer of a band called Joy Division. He killed himself when he was 23."
"Do you think the doctor can use it?"
"Have you ever heard Joy Division? The doctor can use it."

Jon wakes up from his dreams; it is the smallest mercy. He hasn't dared to go out to find more Sadness and the withdrawal is killing him inside. The doctor's voice still echoes in his head, "I will find you." They have to move. They've spent too long here. Jon just has to stay out of his clutches. He tries to forget about it as he stretches and walks around the warehouse. A growing part of him just wants to be alone with his sadness and his memories of Michelle. He hears a scratching noise from one of the side rooms and instantly freezes. With the most hostile illusion he can imagine at the ready, slow dark fire burning over him, he peers round the corner. One Eye is scratching on an old wooden desk with a knife. He's drawing a picture of a park in a small city. There are kids playing with a ball and a family enjoying a picnic and a couple kissing beneath a tree. It's phenomenal.

"That's amazing," says Jon, forgetting his own problems for a moment. It's the first thing that's moved him in years that didn't involve drugs. One Eye doesn't stop, doesn't even register that Jon's there. Jon gets the impression that One Eye always knows what's going on around

en before the things around him do. Jon sits and watches him
inute.

"For an assassin who doesn't talk, you're actually quite a nice guy,
One Eye," says Jon.

One Eye stops and looks at Jon. He scratches with his knife and
writes into the wood, at the bottom, quickly,

MANY ARTISTS ARE NICE PEOPLE.

"Not all artists?" asks Jon.

NO I WOULDN'T SAY THAT. THERE'RE DIFFERENT KINDS OF
ARTISTS AND ONE OF THE KINDS ARE NICE PEOPLE. THEY CREATE
BECAUSE THEY WANT TO DESCRIBE THE WORLD TO OTHERS SO
THAT THEY WON'T MAKE THE SAME MISTAKES OR SO THAT THEY'LL
KNOW WHAT TO LOOK OUT FOR. THEY'RE EXTREME EMPATHS
AND IF YOU'RE EXTREMELY EMPATHIC, YOU'RE EXTREMELY GOOD
AT COMMUNICATING AND ART IS ABOUT COMMUNICATING A
FEELING FROM A THING TO A PERSON. BECAUSE SOMETIMES
THERE ARE NO WORDS FOR FEELINGS. SOMETIMES FEELINGS
CANNOT BE PAINTED OR SUNG. THEY MUST BE DELICATELY
INSCRIBED OR VICIOUSLY CARVED INTO THE THING AND THEN
WHEN SOMEONE HOLDS THAT THING OR LOOKS AT THE THING,
THE FEELING MUST LEAP FROM THE THING TO THE PERSON AND
THEN IT LIVES IN THEIR BRAIN FOREVER.

HOW DOES THIS MAKE GREAT ARTISTS NICE? NICENESS IS
SYMPTOM OF EMPATHY. IT MEANS YOU UNDERSTAND HOW
SOMEONE ELSE FEELS AND IF YOU UNDERSTAND HOW SOMEONE
ELSE FEELS, IT NEARLY ALWAYS MEANS YOU CARE ABOUT THEM
AND IF YOU CARE ABOUT THEM THEN YOU'RE NEARLY ALWAYS
NICE TO THEM.

WHAT ABOUT ARTISTS WHO AREN'T NICE PEOPLE? THEY'RE
JUST NICE PEOPLE WHO CARED TOO MUCH FOR A PERSON OR
A WORLD THAT HURT THEM TOO MUCH. SO NOW THEY CHASE

THE WORLD AND PEOPLE AWAY. OR ELSE, THEY JUST DO TRICKS.
THEY'RE VERY GOOD AT TRICKS AND THAT'S WHAT THEIR ART
IS. TRICKS CAN MAKE YOU LAUGH OR CRY FOR A WHILE BUT NO
TRICK IS FUNNY OR SAD FOREVER. SO I GUESS THOSE ARE GOOD
ARTISTS, NOT GREAT ARTISTS.

A blaze of wood chips follows his carving as his knife finishes slash-
ing the paragraphs of text into the wood. It's the most One Eye has
ever communicated to Jon and for some reason, he's shocked by the
depth of One Eye's opinion. Jon wasn't sure he felt anything at all.

"Were you once a great artist, One Eye, before your vows, before
you were turned into a silencer?" asks Jon.

WAS I A GREAT ARTIST? I DON'T KNOW. HOW DO I FEEL? WE
ARE PRODUCTS OF A MAKER WHO DOES NOT TELL US WHAT WE
ARE SUPPOSED TO BE. HE DOES NOT INCLUDE AN INSTRUCTION
MANUAL. WE MUST GUESS AT THE NEED IN THE WORLD THAT WE
FULFILL, AND THEN DO OUR BEST TO FULFILL IT, TRUSTING THAT
WE ARE DOING THE RIGHT THING WITHOUT EVER KNOWING
BEYOND A SENSE OF PURPOSE IN OUR GUT, THAT WE ARE DOING
THE RIGHT THING.

Jon doesn't understand but he nods and walks off, leaving One Eye
to his art. One Eye was part of a group of protectors and assassins
who spent their lives in the service of others because they'd once done
something so terrible and so unforgivable that they were damned to
spend the rest of their days with their faces and bodies wrapped in
black cloth, their tongues cut out by some cruel Peace Ambassador. It's
an alternative to killing people because there are not many people left
to kill. It had to be chosen, a way to suffer that still allowed the person
suffering to be of some use to society.

Jon had unwittingly saved One Eye's life by breaking down his cell
door during their escape. And now One Eye will be with Jon until he
is indebted to someone else or he dies. He will sleep next to him on
the floor or outside. He will sacrifice his last morsel of food without
thinking about it. He will live, kill, and die for Jon.

Jon does not know this yet. All Jon knows is One Eye reminds him
of a comic book he used to read when he was a child.

CHAPTER 20

NOW

Sylvia Plath's last diary entry. It is packed carefully next to Donald Crowhurt's ship log.

Jon wakes with a start. Visions of the life he and Michelle had or could have had spent the night crashing through his mind. There's a noise. The sound of whispering. The sound of people trying to be quiet and failing. Gravel crunches under a boot somewhere outside. Fuck.

"Edward," whispers Jon and he shoves him. Edward's eyes open almost immediately but Jon holds him tightly and tries with all his might to say what needs to be said with only his eyes: please keep quiet, please, don't say a word and Edward seems to understand. Jon can see flash-lights outside the building; they're being held low but they're there. Jon crawls over to where One Eye should be sleeping but his sleeping bag is empty. Jon hears the first scream. Then gunshots.

Fuck.

Outside, One Eye works his way through a team of five Peace Ambassadors, weaving in and out of the shadows like a snake in tall grass. He throws open the factory door, covered in blood and waves his hands at them, saying without words, 'follow me.' They grab their things and go, running through the streets.

"We can stay with Emily," says Jon.

"Who's Emily?"

"Perhaps the only person we can trust right now."

"I'll take your word for it. And what next?"

"I don't know. I don't care. I need to rest." Edward looks at One Eye and they exchange half a glance. Jon has spent most of the time since the escape sleeping and yet he stills has black rings under his eyes. Edward didn't know him before now but he doubts any human should be like this.

"Ok, we can go to Emily then," says Edward. "Where does she live?"

"In the city. Right next to the ghost of the little girl and her dad the kidnapper," says Jon.

"I know that ghost," says Edward. One Eye nods.

They hide in another warehouse during the day and leave after the sun goes down, keeping to the back streets, not taking the steam train in case they're being watched. The three of them make a motley crew and whenever they get near the general population, Jon immediately creates one of his illusions. They're just three people on their way somewhere else, nothing more.

CHAPTER 21

NOW

Candy. My daughter Candy. Just need the teleporter to work. Just need to get her and then we can go anywhere. The cops will never find us. We'll be happy. So happy. I'll tell her how beautiful her mom was and I'll tell her she's just as beautiful. I'll keep her safe. I'll tell her everything I know about the world, every poem, every joke, every place I've ever heard about and we can be happy. We will eat sugar and grapefruit, she loves sugar and grapefruit. I will make her pray before each meal, her mother would've liked that. There she is. Pick her up. Cops. Cops. Cops. My shoulder. My shoulder on fire. Gunshot. Must protect Candy. Doesn't matter if I die. Must protect Candy. Get her through the teleporter. Candy. My daughter Candy. Just need the teleporter to work. Just need to get her and then we can go anywhere. The cops will never find us.

She, miles away, still has bright blue eyes that sparkle in the haze of the dying sun above. She works in an algae farm now with other The End orphans. It's all she's ever known since The End. She's barefoot and her feet are cracked and tough from running through the fields and working on the old copper machines that process the algae, that bubble steam through the green soupy vats, which are then harvested and transmuted into a variety of different meals that are then beamed to the MicroPVRs of the people lucky enough to live in NewLand.

A plane flies overhead then touches down at the abandoned airfield.

It's the commercial flight. The last running plane on the planet. She hasn't seen an airplane in years. When she last saw one, it was during one of the wars, during the chaos of one of the exoduses from the forgotten place she's now in. One of the imperial captains of the United Government smashed his wedding implant against the wrist of his orphaned, peasant-girl lover, instantly binding them, which allowed her onto the departing plane to escape this hell.

She'd felt so much envy when that happened; but now, some part of her she thought long gone sparkles and fades inside. It feels like hope but only just.

CHAPTER 22

NOW

A son falls asleep in his dying father's arms and the last
thing he sees before he closes his eyes is a tattoo of a
heart with his mother's name written across it.

"Give us your credits, fools, and you might make it out of this alive,"
says the little one. The three thugs think they can take the three strangers with hoods pulled low, especially looking at Jon. Thin, weak Jon.
Jon knows this pattern. He's seen it all his life. He's so weak, Edward
is holding him now. He needs Sadness. He needs Michelle. He needs
Emily. He doesn't need this.

"You're making a mistake. You should leave," says Jon. Edward
growls under his breath and one of the big ones takes a step towards
Jon. One Eye, on the other hand, explodes.

His body arcs through the air and seems to escape time for a second,
like a frozen glint of light off a distant sword. And then his body comes
crashing down into the thugs towering over Jon. For a moment things
are still as the thugs try to work out what the black, lithe shadow in
front of them is. One of the big ones opens his mouth for a second,
managing only a guttural choking noise instead of the "Get him!" he
intends, as a blade secreted somewhere in the shadow before him finds
his throat. The other big one has a Charge Club™ and he swings it,
sparks shooting from it in pulses, at where the shadow is supposed to
be but isn't. He hits only air. The shadow raises his foot as he steps and
kicks the Charge Club™ along, adding momentum to its swing and
making it smash, sickeningly, into the jaw of the thug next to him. The

shadow dips and rises once again and before he knows it, the thug with the Charge Club™ dies, a sharp pain behind his neck the only clue as to why or how.

Now only the little one remains. Eyes wide and no big ones left, he flees, leaving the dead bodies and the three strangers behind.

"Run," breathes Edward under his hood, holding Jon. And they do, Edward helping Jon every step of the way.

"Stop, please fucking stop," Jon says, several city blocks later, collapsing against Edward. Edward looks up; Jon's fallen against a makeshift cafe made out of old corrugated iron. An old, bent-over man with a thick mop of grey hair comes up to them and waves his hand at them to beckon them.

"Come inside, please, you must be hungry." Edward looks at Jon and he nods. Something, besides the fact that he's being so friendly to three out-of-breath strangers, doesn't seem quite right about the old man but Jon can't pin it down.

The old man seats them at the lone table inside and gives them all menus. Jon hasn't seen a menu in ten years. All his food just comes out of the MicroPVR. He tries to focus on it. It feels so alien, to be looking at a menu now and for some reason, he welcomes it. It's a part of a world long gone. Edward and One Eye are scanning the outside door for more thugs or Peace Patrols but slowly they relax.

"I haven't thought about food in ages," says Edward.

"I didn't even know you ate food. I though you just lived off sunlight," says Jon, only half joking.

"No, I can do that if I want to but I enjoy eating. It reminds me of what I was like before." Edward looks away at something not visible to the rest of them before carrying on, "I used to eat everything: pizzas, hamburgers, spaghetti, even salads although for some reason that seems a bit wrong these days." Jon manages a laugh. The old man comes back to their table.

"Do you know what you want?"

"Yes," Jon points at the lasagna on the menu. The old man doesn't react. That's what's wrong, thinks Jon. He's blind. No wonder he's serving them. No one would normally serve a half-ent or a silencer.

"I'll have the lasagna," says Jon.

"As will we," says Edward. He looks across at One Eye and One

Eye nods.

"Excellent," says the old man and he takes their menus. He returns a minute later with three bowls of soup.

"This isn't what we asked for," says Jon. He doesn't want to upset the old man but maybe he's just made a mistake.

"I know. You wanted lasagna. But I don't have lasagna. I just have soup. I just wanted to know what you wanted, in case it was soup," says the old man.

"What kind of soup is it?" asks Edward.

"It's just soup," says the old man.

"It doesn't have a name?" asks Edward.

"Do you?" asks the old man with a smile on his face.

"Thank you," says Jon, interrupting quickly. He and Edward look at each other and Edward starts laughing softly to himself behind his hand. Jon finds himself struggling to contain his own laughter. Suddenly, One Eye's hand shoots out and grabs his wrist. Jon looks at him. One Eye is scrawling on the table with his knife.

You must remember this feeling, Jon.

"What feeling?"

The feeling of being happy. It doesn't happen often but when it does, you must grab it with both hands and hold it close. Let it overwhelm you. Don't over-analyse any emotion. But remember it. Always remember it.

Edward looks over at what One Eye has written and asks the question both Jon and he have had on their minds.

"Who are you, One Eye?" One Eye slowly returns his knife to the table and starts carving out words.

Just a man who made a mistake. And like all mistakes, it must be paid for. My servitude is that payment.

Jon and Edward don't say anymore and they finish their soup together in silence, only broken by Edward's occasionally slurping.

"Let's go," says Edward after they're done and they get up to leave.

"How much do we owe you?" asks Jon to the old man, who gets up to see them out the door.

"Nothing," says the old man. "I feed anyone who comes here." It's strange that while this man seems happy, Jon thinks, he doesn't seem to have the chemically induced grin and haze across his eyes common to the rest of the population.

"Thank you. I must ask one more thing of you," says Jon.

"Yes?"

"You must tell no one we were here."

"I know."

"You know?"

"I know who you and your half-ent and your silencer friend are. I don't know your names or what you've done but I know you're good people and that's enough. I am not as blind as I look. And I can still feel things. Even here, in the dark." He suddenly reaches out and grabs Jon's hand, holding it tightly and his blind eyes seem to stare into Jon's soul.

"The point is to remember. You should listen to your mute friend. This is all a dream. You will come this way again." The voice doesn't sound like it belongs to him.

Jon backs away slowly and they leave the strange shop. Jon is too tired to question the old man's words.

They carry on. When they finally get to Emily's house, Jon slams his hands on the front door. They're answered only by silence and a distant neighbour yelling at them to shut up.

"Emily," says Jon against the door.

"No one's inside," says Edward looking through one of the windows. Below them, the ghost of the little girl and her father the kidnapper are shot at, again and again, by the same police as always. Nothing changes.

"She must be at the club," says Jon. He stumbles and holds himself up against the side of the building, growing weak. The soup helped but he needs his Sadness.

"What club?"

"Cabaret du Néant," says Jon.

"That's not a club, that's a front for Duer and his drug money," says Edward, spitting on the ground.

"I guess everyone really does know," says Jon.

"It's the worst-kept secret ever, I think even the fleas know," says

Edward. One Eye hangs back from the conversation.

"Let's go," says Jon.

"Go to Cabaret du Néant? You think we're going to find safe haven there?" asks Edward.

"I don't know, Edward, but maybe they'll let me sleep," says Jon, snapping just a little.

"Fine. Let's go," says Edward, brushing off Jon's increasingly strange behavior, and they head off into the shadows of the city.

CHAPTER 23

NOW

I'm sorry, Jon. I thought we were doing the right thing.
I can feel the blackness coming. I can feel the shadows
crawling up and out of my skin. I know I'm killing the world
and I'm sorry. I can feel my body dying. I think of the things
that protect you, Jon. I think of the oak tree and your
comic books. I think of the things that protect you as I die.
I'm so sorry. I will always love you. I will always love you.
I will....

"Where's Emily?" asks Jon, and Barnston wakes with a start, nearly falling off his stool and sending his top hat tumbling. The barman looks up from the glasses he's polishing and he eyes Jon up and down. Then he does the same to Jon's friends. It's late afternoon and the Cabaret hasn't opened yet but the doors still recognised Jon's biometrics and they let him in, even without his wrist implant.

"You haven't shown up for a performance in days and then you just appear, out of the blue, asking questions you expect me to answer?" says Barnston. "How about you answer some of my questions first?"

Jon's barely hanging on to consciousness, his mind is reeling and his muscles ache with every breath he takes.

"Just tell me where Emily is, Barnston," says Jon, again, this time a little more forcefully. Edward pulls back his hood and un-hunches his shoulders, rustling his leaves and giving Barnston and the barman an idea of just how big he really is. The club has half-ent bouncers of its own but none of them are at work yet. The barman looks at Edward, then at Jon and then slowly his gaze falls on One Eye, standing at the back. He shrugs. None of it really matters to him.

Barnston sighs, puts his head in his hands and speaks through his fingers, "Fuck it, I've got bigger acts than you. She's in the back with Duer. She owes him money so I'd be careful what you say in there, he's not in the best of moods."

Before he's even finished talking, Jon is making his way to the back where Duer keeps court with the Geisslerlieder, his clan, and personal army: the ones who control the flow of Sadness through the city.

He throws open the door marked Staff Only and on a makeshift wooden throne, a man with long curly black hair looks up, surprised at the disturbance. The packed room of thugs, assassins, and thieves looks at Jon and his friends.

"I'm already killing one person today, I can easily make it four. Tell me who you are so that my assistants know what to write on your gravestone," says the man who Jon assumes must be Duer.

"I'm Jon, this is Edward and One Eye," says Jon as the others fill the room.

"Really? That's fascinating. I do know who you are then. Mainly because of that," says Duer, pointing towards the edge of the dark hall. Jon's eyes have been adjusting to the light but things have gotten clearer. A naked, bald and pale man covered in tattoos of 1s and 0s from head to toe is lying up against a wall, quite dead, disemboweled and quartered, violently.

"Jesus," says Edward looking over Jon's shoulder.

"No, we believe his name was Gerald. Or at least that was one of the words he screamed before he died," says Duer.

"What's he got to do with us?" asks Jon.

"Besides the fact you might die in a similar manner? This man was one of the United Government's new universal messengers and he was carrying a message about you."

"What's a universal messenger?" asks Edward.

"You are an inquisitive shrub. The theory goes that if you want to transmit an absolutely ridiculous amount of data and be absolutely sure no one's going intercept it, you use one of these guys. He is, or at least was, a human flash drive."

"That's ridiculous, there's no way those 1s and 0s tattooed on him could hold more than a few kilobytes of data," say Jon.

"You are correct and an idiot at the same time, which is a strange combination. The 1s and 0s are merely the encryption method, the password if you will. The data is encoded into his DNA itself."

"How do you get the password?" asks Edward.

Duer grins like a Cheshire cat. "Well, there's the easy way and the hard way. The easy way is if you're the person the data is intended for, the messenger simply willingly steps into a specially designed photo booth, naked, and is then photographed. The 1s and 0s are collated and entered as a password, a piece of hair or a drop of spit or whatever contains his DNA is taken from the messenger and the information is extracted. The messenger goes home and has a nice cup of tea. Then there's the hard way. The hard way is five of my boys drop down off the roof into a dark alley the messenger happens to be walking through and they beat the ever-loving fuck out of him, without tearing his skin or damaging any of the tattoos. Then the messenger, unwillingly, is divided up into pieces and his entire body is photographed individually. The code on his body is then written down into one long password and we take whatever's left of him to make a DNA sample. We extract the information from that sample and then enter the password. Simple really," says Duer, cleaning his nails while he explains this.

"I still don't understand what this has to do with us," says Jon.

"This is what his DNA contained," says Duer and he motions with his hand at one of his lackeys, who pushes play on a holo-projector.

The room is suddenly filled with objects with writing on them—diaries, guitars, screenshots, rocks, photographs—and in the centre of all this are three-dimensional representations of Jon, One Eye and Edward.

"I know you're important gentlemen, especially if you're important to the government, I just don't know why yet," says Duer.

Jon pays special attention to the fact that the room is filled with Duer's thugs and pushers. He has no doubt that the three of them could probably take them all on but he still doesn't know where Emily is and he suddenly feels their roles reverse. He came here so she could save him. Now, he'll have to save her.

"I've got news that may impact not just your little gang of thugs here, Duer, but perhaps the entire world. The United Government wants to make The End happen, again."

Duer looks up and a silence falls over those assembled in his back alley throne room.

"What do you mean? My parents died in The End. I would advise not lying to me or messing me around on this one," says Duer and his feigned disinterest is replaced by a hint of steel in his voice.

"I'm not. I can tell you what they're planning but first we need to see Emily," says Jon.

"Emily? That little whore owes me more money than she can count," says Duer and Jon has to stop himself from using the last of his fading energy to charge the throne.

A thought suddenly strikes Jon. It almost kills him. He hasn't paid Emily for the Sadness she's been feeding him for months now. She's never brought it up. There's every chance he's the reason she's in this mess. The thought is cold and hard and slices through the mush that Jon's brain has become in its withdrawn state.

"The information I give you will be worth whatever she owes you," says Jon. Duer sits and thinks for a moment.

"Very well. Let's talk in my private chambers," says Duer and he snaps his fingers. The thugs make a path from him to a wooden door at the back of the room. Duer goes to it, opens it and waits for Jon to join him.

"Just him, you two can stay outside," says Duer and One Eye immediately starts to draw a blade from somewhere.

"Stop, One Eye," says Jon. "Let me talk to him, I'll be fine."

One Eye seems to strain against himself but he puts the blade back. The thugs around him breathe a collective sigh of relief. Jon and Duer step inside. Jon wonders what tattoos Gerald would've chosen, if he had a choice.

CHAPTER 24

NOW

Elsewhere are two letters that were never sent,
because of pride, each a declaration of love
that would've changed lives.

Here, the room is like a library but instead of books, hundreds of vials hang from hooks around the room, each with a label attached to it.

Rose Cottage, Dutch Tears, Snow Dawn, Saudade, Limerence, Ubi Sunt, Memento Mori, Crowhurst, Stendhal Syndrome, Lazarus Syndrome, Sic Transit Gloria Mundi, Melencolia, Lamentation, Judgement, La Petite Mort, Moriendo Renascor, Isaiah 22, Pie Jesu, Requiem, Ad Mortem Festinamus, The Wild, Fimbulwinter…

Jon's mind slowly comprehends that every single one is a different form of Sadness.

Duer turns to him, "Booze makes you stupid and like it. It makes you fall around and not care. And eventually, stupid is the only way you know how to be. Cocaine makes you feel important, that life matters, that you matter. That the music is better than it really is. That every conversation is profound and that all pretenses have been stripped away. Ecstasy makes you dance all night and love your friends so much, in a way that you've never been able to tell them about before. Acid makes you see pretty colours and makes things breathe. But Sadness, there is nothing like Sadness."

Duer goes to the shelves and holds up the vials one by one.

"This one feels like a death in the family, whomever you're closest to and it makes you remember every good time you shared that you'll never have again. It tastes like old age and bitterness and regret, like a phone not ringing. This one feels like your God has abandoned you and that you're truly alone in the universe. It makes your mind so dark and so cold that your soul wants to scream. This one is the bitterest. It tastes like squandered talent and this one is the subtlest, it tastes like a lover turning away from you and makes you hear the words 'we need to talk' in the back of your mind. It makes you feel like someone's, casually, leaving you forever. It's obvious and blunt but it takes a real connoisseur to appreciate the nuances. This one feels like apathy and wanting to leave your skin. This one feels like a desire to fix something which can never be fixed. This one makes you feel like your dog has died. The one you've had since it was a puppy. Exactly like that. It's considered a novelty by some. This one feels like a conversation not had. This one feels like yourself yelling at yourself."

"It's quite a collection," says Jon and he fights the urge to smash one of the vials open and immediately swallow it. The feeling is like an unholy typhoon inside him, begging to be let out. He starts to sweat.

"I'm quite a collector. I'm glad you can appreciate it," says Duer. "Would you like some?" He offers Jon a vial and Jon's hands shake as he takes it. Jon pours some of it into his mouth. The familiar feelings begin to overtake him. Somewhere else, he's back with Michelle and they're happy again; he's happy, in his sadness. Everything is normal.

"Whoa, take it easy, trickster," says Duer as Jon falls to the floor, emptying the bottle. Jon is somewhere else. Jon is somewhere else. Jon is somewhere else. Somewhere, with Michelle.

CHAPTER 25

NOW

A son makes himself a birthday card each year his father isn't there and pretends it's from him. He turns twenty and throws them all away. But someone finds them.

"Get the hell up," says Emily and she pours a bucket of water over Jon's face. Jon is yanked back to reality, back from the place where he and Michelle are real again, back to this hell without her.

"What the fuck is wrong with you?" asks Jon as he looks around and he knows that there's probably less wrong with her than there is with him. Edward is there. One Eye is there. Duer is there, with his personal honour guard of thugs.

"I've never seen an addiction as strong as yours," says Duer. "You're lucky you're still alive. Your friends here bargained for your life and they've managed to convince me that what you have to say is worth hearing. I hope, for your sake, that they're right," says Duer, pacing slowly across the room.

Jon finds some remaining human part of himself and he turns to Emily. "Are you alright?" For the first time in a while, there's genuine human emotion in his voice, there's feeling and there's caring. Emily manages a smile.

"I'm alright," she says and she means as much of that as she can.

"You've been asleep for a while. I believe it'd be best if you start talking," says Duer.

"Fine, but in private," says Jon.

"Fine with me but no more Sadness for you until this is over," says

Duer and Jon nods, ignoring the lump in his throat, the animal, the typhoon inside him screaming for more and more and more.

"Emily, you need to hear this too. Duer, bring your most trusted men in with you, everyone else must stay outside," says Jon. They walk back into Duer's study and One Eye and Edward take their place outside it, discouraging any eavesdroppers. And Jon, in that little room, explains how his father ended the world.

CHAPTER 26

NOW

A single tear on a post-it note that says, "Goodbye forever.
I will love you for just as long."

"You're lying," says Duer and he slams his fist against the table. "I
know what I saw, I know what killed my parents."

"Do you really?" asks Jon, "Ask your men, one at a time, what they
saw. Was it an earthquake? A nuclear holocaust? An invading army? The
only common denominator is the shadows, that's it."

"If what you're saying is true, then it's the greatest lie ever told,"
says Duer. He stares out the window at the distant marble spires of the
United Government building. Jon can tell some part of him is starting to believe. Emily is crying in the corner. Duer's two top men are
whispering quickly to each other, debating Jon's story.

"And you say this doctor you encountered, he wants to do it again?"

"Yes, he says the illusion wasn't finished at The End, that because my
father died, he never completed the second part," says Jon.

"What's the second part?"

"I don't know exactly. I think because the first part was catastrophe,
depression and misery, the second part was supposed to be some kind
of positive hallucination, something that pulled everyone together and
inspired them to fight a common enemy to build a better world. But
that's just a guess."

"The doctor needs you, right?"

"Yes, that's what he said."

"Well then, my little friends, all we need to do is keep you out of his hands for a few days and we've won, correct?"

"Correct. There's something about the significance of the date that it happened last time, it makes the illusion powerful, something about the emotional resonance everyone has with it. He can try and use me after it but it won't work nearly as well. He believes that he needs me on that date, as near as I can tell," says Jon. Duer steeples his hands in thought, then after a pause, claps them.

"Very well, we will hide you and your friends from the United Government, at least until the anniversary of The End passes."

"Thank you," says Jon. The animal inside him is screaming for more. He reaches out for another vial of Sadness.

"May I?" he says.

Duer makes a mock bow and says, "Go right ahead."

Emily looks away. She knows she helped make Jon the addict that he is. And now, she's starting to regret it.

CHAPTER 27

NOW

A woman turns away from the man she loves, as a passerby takes a picture. The picture is saved on a memory card.

Emily hears Jon's voice talking in the small room Duer gave him to sleep in. No one's responding. At least, no one living. She opens the door.

"Jon?" He doesn't answer. "Jon?" She asks again, into the darkness.

"What do you want?" comes the voice, weak and feeble.

"What's wrong with you?" Emily asks, sitting down on the edge of his bed.

"What's wrong with me? I don't know, my father's responsible for Armageddon and apparently I could be, too; everyone insists the girl I've been in love with for the last ten years of my life doesn't even exist; and I'm living in a store room belonging to one of the most powerful drug dealers in the city. Other than that, nothing is wrong with me."

Emily could hear him opening another vial of Sadness in the darkness.

"Jesus, Jon, how much of that do you really need?"

"Every time I take it, it brings her back to me, Emily. It brings Michelle back," Jon laments.

"She's not real, Jon. She's a construction." A vial flies across the room and smashes against the wall behind Emily's head.

"She's not a construction," says Jon and she can hear his voice shaking. He's full of fullstops and anger.

"Michelle, don't listen to her, she doesn't know what she's talking about." Suddenly, a soft glow fills the room and Michelle appears next to Jon, bathing his forehead in water, wiping it with a cloth.

"She's not real, Jon, no matter what you do, no matter how real you try and make her," says Emily. Michelle's ghost looks at her with scorn in her eyes.

"I know your eyes are behind hers, Jon, even if you don't," says Emily and she turns to leave the room. Jon screams and the room is bathed in imaginary flames as he retreats to his imaginary lover. Emily shuts the door behind her and leaves Jon in a purgatory of his own design.

An hour later, she finds him in the bar, drunk.

"Talk to me, Jon."

"Why can't I just be quiet? Why can't I just be quiet and happy? Why do I have to be making a noise for you to be happy? Don't you fucking get how upset making noise makes me? Don't you fucking get it? I just want to be ok. That's all I fucking want."

Emily doesn't take his shit, she repeats herself: "Jon, talk to me."

And he cries in that way that only addicts can, in that way that only the people who will always know what it means to always be wanting something they cannot have.

Jon talks about his drug, "There's not a breath of air I can breathe or a step I can take that won't remind me of her. She is as much a part of me as my skin."

Emily sits next to him and puts her hand on his shoulder.

"But she was never real, Jon."

"She was real to me. And while I can be logical about this, logic has never once mended a broken heart or fixed a sundered soul. She has poisoned the very core of me. A dream has killed me."

Emily pulls him closer, putting her arms around him and feeling something for him she hasn't felt since she was a teenager.

He whispers into her ear, "Perhaps I can live through this. But I would be deluding myself if I thought that late at night, before I slept, she wouldn't return to haunt me. And that would be unfair to whomever I was trying to sleep next to. No matter how pure my intentions were. There are no soulmates. Love is a lie. Love, is broken."

Something about the way Jon says this breaks him; and a little of it breaks Emily inside, too.

CHAPTER 28

NOW

An executioner's mask.

Jon tries to sleep but all he can do is remember; he remembers what it was like to touch her, when he first thought she was real, her skin was a foreign land he'd never finish exploring, a place where he'd always be a welcome stranger but a stranger nonetheless. His fingers would travel from her neck, down her back, across her ribs, and if they were in bed, slowly towards her thighs, always moving, just above her skin.

And she would sigh softly and welcome him into her land.

Jon screams himself to sleep.

Emily can hear it in the next room.

"You need to stop giving him Sadness, Duer," says Emily. Duer smiles.

He knew this was coming.

"He's a big boy, Emily. I also don't think you're in a position to be giving me orders," says Duer.

"He's going to kill himself or all of us if you keep feeding him that stuff," she says.

"I'm sorry, Miss Emily, but last I checked you were the one who got him started on the stuff," and as he says it, Emily clenches her jaw.

"I know. It was a mistake."

"That's the thing about mistakes Emily, my dear, is that you have to live with them. We all do."

"I'm not even sure why you're helping him, Duer."

"It's simple, Emily. Power. If even half of what he says is true, he could change the world as we know it. Don't you think the world needs changing?"

"Maybe. I guess it depends on what you want to change it to," says Emily.

Duer walks across the room to her and runs his fingers through her hair. She noticeably cringes at his touch and as she pulls away, he wraps her hair in his hand and yanks her head closer to him.

"When you're me, darling, you can change the world to whatever you want." She starts to cry. There's a knock on the door.

"Boss?" one of the thugs asks, the door half opens.

"What is it, you fool? Can't you see I'm busy?" Duer snarls from across the room.

"There's someone here to see her," says the thug.

"Who?"

"Her," says the thug and he points at Emily. Emily has no one left in this world. And yet, here was someone. Duer lets go of her hair, losing interest in her like a cat losing interest in a dead bird.

"Go," he says and waves her away, still sobbing.

She walks outside towards the bar and meets a ghost.

CHAPTER 29

NOW

Hemingway's shotgun

"Emily thought this would be good for you," says Edward. They're in the back of one of Duer's delivery carriages, hidden behind boxes of old bottles and crates and other things they'd piled on top to hide themselves from the city's Peace Patrols. It's the night before the anniversary of The End.

They just have to stay out of the clutches of the doctor for another 24 hours and everything will be ok. Or at least, as ok as it was going to get. They can never go back to normal, whatever that once was.

"I still don't know where we're going, Edward," says Jon. He raises another vial of Sadness to his lips and drains it. It takes more and more to actually have any kind of effect on him, to feel anything at all.

"You'll see," says Edward. And he smiles. He thinks One Eye is smiling, too. Even in the dark, he can sense a change in the mood. The carriage rattles along, past smoke stacks and broken homes, past schools and factories for what feels like forever. Finally, it stops.

"We're here," says Edward. The driver goes round the back and opens up for them and they find themselves in a blasted, desolate suburb that looks like it's been looted more times than the sun has risen. Jon looks around him, then he recognises some of the architecture of the house next to them. It's the home he grew up in. Jon runs inside. There's his room. There's his parents' room, beneath the graffiti and burned out walls; this is where he became what he became. This is where he snuck out that night with Emily and Michelle and here, here is the bathroom where his mother killed herself soon after The End. He touches the wall and steadies himself.

"Why did you bring me here?" he asks, staring into the closed lids of his eyes.

"Emily said it might remind you of who you once were, before you became this mess, before Michelle, before The End, before anything."

Jon walks outside and One Eye and Edward follow him. Here is the road they walked down together. At the end is a park. The park where they swung and smoked and this is the place Jon last felt normal. Jon starts to retrace the steps he took ten years ago. He turns and he's facing the park. Only one swing remains, the rest are all stolen or burnt. On that swing is a woman. Jon feels like he should know her. She's familiar yet different. He walks up to her and she turns around and stands up as he approaches.

"Hello, Jon," says Michelle.

CHAPTER 30

NOW

Steven's hands were soft, yet he worked with them all the time. Hands made for praying and now he's dead. Now he's dead and I am alone. I am alone. I will fall off this building and I will hit the ground so fast, I will fly into his arms on the other side. He will read to me each night we spend in heaven. His voice will be the last thing I hear. I will never hear silence again. He will write his name and then the word "loves" and then my name on my skin with his fingers. I will fall and then I will fly and then I will be with him. We will be together again soon and I will hold his hand and he will hold mine. Jump now. Now. Now. Now.

Steven's hands were soft, yet he worked with them all the time. Hands made for praying and now he's dead. Now he's dead and I am alone.

It doesn't make sense. A part of Jon's brain always lights up whenever Michelle is around but not now. Now she's just here and if he blinks, she doesn't stop existing and when she talks, Jon has never thought of the words she's saying. She is her own entity. Her own person. Not Jon's.

"I managed to finally find my way off the algae farm and back to the city and I ran into one or two people I used to know, they told me I could find Emily at that club and she told me what had happened, to a greater or lesser extent, and now I'm here," says Michelle.

Jon still hasn't processed it completely. She's Michelle but she's not his Michelle. Her hips are slightly rounder, her hair isn't silver anymore, more brown. She is not hanging on his every word. She is not a figment of his imagination. This is the real Michelle. Jon nods at the things she says, his brain slowly turning things over. Edward and One Eye have given them some privacy and are standing at the back of the park, keeping an eye out for looters or wandering Peace Ambassadors.

"I don't know who I've become," says Jon.

"I don't think I know either, if you're looking for an answer. I met you *once*, Jon. I didn't expect you to form a relationship with someone you thought was me."

"I didn't know she wasn't you. I didn't know she was just some lonely part of me."

"I understand. Kind of. I think." They sit in silence for a moment.

"Come here," says Michelle and Jon gets up and hugs her like he loves her.

"I'm sorry," she whispers in his ear as she touches the edge of a Charge Stick™ to the side of his neck. Jon shakes uncontrollably and with his last moments of consciousness, he sees a phalanx of Peace Officers walk around the edge of the park up to him and Michelle. She holds him as he falls. The last thing he hears as he passes out are the yells of Edward and One Eye as a thousand shots ring out.

CHAPTER 31

NOW

Mary. I'm alive. I didn't die. Don't jump off the building, Mary. I love you more than anything else. I don't want to bury you. Please, Mary. Don't do it. Stay with me. We can be happy while we're here. We've got years left. We've got so many seconds left to hold each other. Please, Mary.

Mary. I'm alive. I didn't die. Don't jump off the building. Mary. I love you more than anything else. I don't want to bury you. Please, Mary.

When Jon comes to, the room he's in is quiet except for the whir of sextants tracking the stars and the crackle of the fire that powers them. Long curtains hang from the ceiling, hiding more spinning machines and through two of them, Jon can see the lights of the last city on Earth blinking like distant white skulls. Michelle is there. The real one. She's in a government uniform, a red one he hasn't seen before. It is exactly ten years to the day that The End began.

"What job did they offer you in exchange for betraying me?"

"This is my Auto Systemic Meridian Response uniform."

"It's cute."

"It's the uniform one wears when one whispers quietly and performs small tasks for the benefit of government employees, so that they may experience a tingling sensation across their skull. If someone draws you, or whispers softly near you, this is the tiny shiver you get, the pleasurable tingling sensation across your scalp and back. It is called ASMR for short. The experience has become a delicacy amongst government employees."

"That's all it took to betray me? A job as someone who whispers softly to others to give them goosebumps?"

"You don't know what I've been through, Jon."

"I know you better than you think."

"No you don't. You know some fantastical version of me you've built in your head. You know a sixteen year old girl that you met once. Every single other thing about me that you think you know, you've made up."

"No, there are parts of you that were real."

"No, Jon, there weren't. I don't even like comic books. I just told you I liked comic books that night because I thought you were kind of cute."

"You lied to me?"

"Yes, Jon, ten years ago, when I was a kid, I lied to you and I'm sorry that hurts you."

"This isn't you."

"This is me. You've been in love with a ghost for ten years, Jon; an illusion, an imaginary friend and I'm sorry to be the one to tell you this but that girl never existed anywhere but your head."

"You don't know what you're saying, what we've shared."

"Don't you fucking get it, you fucking weirdo? We haven't shared anything. I've been working on a goddamn algae farm for ten years in the middle of fucking nowhere. I saw you once, one night before The End and then my parents died, and I was shipped off to one of the new United Government orphan work camps and that was it. You are nothing to me!"

"You don't mean that."

"Yes I do, Jon, yes I do. I don't even know who you are." There's silence for a while as everything that's been said slowly becomes real.

"I'm sorry," she whispers and turns away.

"Never apologise for how you feel," says Jon softly, more to himself than to her.

"What?"

"I said never apologise for how you feel. No one can control how they feel. The sun doesn't apologise for being the sun. The rain doesn't say sorry for falling. Feelings just are," says Jon.

Michelle walks across to where he's facing the dark curtains and the city and reaches out touch him on the shoulder, once, for real. She pulls her hand back at the last second and turns away, coming face to face with herself and she takes in air sharply.

"Michelle, this is Michelle," says Jon. "The person you could've been."

The differences are small but striking. Jon's Michelle has perfect hair, a perfect body and a perfect face. She smiles at the real Michelle, who is only human.

"This isn't me, Jon. This is a cardboard cutout."

Michelle walks to the door and the doctor's personal Peace Officers enter and grab Jon roughly by the arms. Jon's Michelle disappears.

"You're not getting away this time, you tricksy fucking bastard," says one.

Jon no longer cares. Jon will throw himself over the edge of the building if he gets the chance. There is nothing and no one left to live for. He will join his father and mother on the other side. If there is one.

Perhaps feeling nothing is better than feeling this.

CHAPTER 32

NOW

A single rusted nail, more than 2,000 years old.

Edward and One Eye are strapped to the wall at the far end of a cell.

"Christ all-bloody mighty, those tranq guns fucking hurt. I've got bruises on my bruises. I can't believe that Michelle bitch betrayed us, why the hell would anyone love her? Even the ghost of her. Sometimes I think Jon's a bit of idiot," says Edward. He trails off for a moment as his eyes roll around, still slightly dizzy from the tranqs the Peace Officers shot them with. "You know, One Eye, you're not that bad for someone who doesn't say a word. Although I think that might be why I like you. Everyone else is always talking, talking and you, you just shut up and listen. Would you like to hear the story of how I became a tree?"

"Shut the hell up in there," says the guard from outside.

"Come in here and make me, you daft arsehat," replies Edward.

The door opens and the guard steps inside. That is his second mistake. The first is not making sure that he tightened One Eye's cuffs properly. Or at least, made them so tight that even if One Eye did dislocate his thumb, which he did, he wouldn't be able to get his hand out, which he does. The guard, unaware that the assassin on the wall to the left of him is now free, walks up to Edward to teach the half-tree a lesson. He opens his mouth to tell Edward what he's going to do to him but never gets that far; One Eye snaps his neck like a dry twig.

"Come on, we need to find Jon and get the hell out of here," says Edward. One Eye points to one of the heating vents outside.

"Ok, let's try that," says Edward and he walks up to the grate and lifts it off. He and One Eye disappear inside.

"I hope you know where you're going, One Eye," says Edward and One Eye nods back, in the dark.

They travel for a few minutes before they start to hear voices coming from below. Edward recognises the doctor's. He's filed it away in a special place in his brain and marked it for future reference. It's a voice he wants to remove from the face of the planet. He raises his fist to slam through the vent below them and attack but One Eye grabs his wrist and stops him. Edward's eyes are wide but One Eye keeps holding his wrist and tries desperately to sign his intent to Edward. He puts his fingers in front of his lips and cups his other hand to his ear. Edward has never been the type to stop and listen before he acts but every day he spends with Jon and One Eye teaches him something new. He slowly relaxes his grip and One Eye does the same with his. They listen.

"...and we've got more than enough Sadness, our men raided Duer's hideout and took his entire stockpile. He and his goons are all dead."

"Good. He would've become a problem at some point anyway. And the machine? Is the machine ready?"

"Yes, we've updated it slightly to accept different media formats but essentially it'll function the same way it did ten years ago. Because of the previous escape, we've doubled our security forces and brought in twenty elite Peace Angels and several Assault Seraphim."

"Excellent. We're going to change the world today. We'd best do it properly."

One Eye looks through the grill in the vent and does his best to work out how exactly the machine works. There is a series of pictures being displayed on a screen next to it and a nurse is saving some and discarding others. There are strange objects on a tray next to her and several boxes of Sadness piled high in the corner and what looks like a captain of the guard and several scientists talking to the doctor.

This is going to be tricky. He reaches across to Edward, grabs his hand and starts tracing letters on his palm in the dark. Edward starts to shake One Eye off before he realises what One Eye is trying to do. In the dark, letter by letter, One Eye tells Edward what's going to happen if they use Jon like they used his father.

CHAPTER 33

NOW

"What's this?"
"It's a napkin used by the saddest girl in the world to dry
her tears."
"Let me guess. Sylvia Plath?"
"No, no one famous. But we knew about her. She gave off
so much resonance it turned our entire map black for one
city block."
"And she was no one special?"
"You wouldn't recognise her name if I told it to you."
"So just an everyday, normal person carrying her shopping,
reading books at night and going for drinks occasionally
with her friends, just some person, that's the saddest girl
in the world?"
"Yes. Just a regular person."

The door to Jon's cell burst open and Edward and One Eye step in, one after the other, covered in blood, none of which appears to be theirs.

"I never want to spend that much time in a heating vent ever again," Edward says as he throws the dead body of a guard next to Jon. Jon doesn't move. There's no point anymore.

"Snap out of it," says Edward and he shakes Jon to try and get him to react. Edward's sense of humour is finally depleted.

"Jon, there's a good chance we're not going to make it out of this. They're ready for us this time. They've got a small army outside. We need to have a plan ready in case they do to you whatever they did to your father. Jon? Are you listening to me? We need you to save the world," Edward shakes him some more.

Jon is practically a dead weight. One Eye slams his fist into the wall behind them to get his attention and frantically shakes him some more. The screens in the room flicker on, bright white, blinding Edward. They start filling up with text; it's the same words over and over again: "You have read this all before and you will again. You have read this all before and you will again." Jon finally focuses on him. And he laughs.

"What the fuck are you doing? Jon?"

"I don't know, Edward. My head, it feels like it's leaking into the machines, into the tiles, into the books, everything's leaking out of my head."

"You need to snap out of it, Jon, we need you to stop that asshole from killing what's left of the human race. We need you to save the world."

"Save the world, Edward? The world that killed my father? That drove my mother to kill herself? That would make me fall in love with a dream?"

"That's not the world, Jon. That's just what happened and you can't blame the entire world for what happened to you."

"Then whom do I blame, Edward?"

"Sometimes, Jon, there's no one left to blame. Sometimes, things just happen. We need you. Now."

He's holding Jon's hand, pressing something into it but Jon can't feel anything outside himself.

More guards are on the way. The screens flicker off and on, repeating the same phrases over and over and they slow, like a heartbeat. Things are desperate. Edward is desperate and he doesn't have time to do this with Jon, to pull him back from the brink.

"I've never actually loved anyone, Edward," says Jon.

"Shut the fuck up, Jon, you need to stay here, in this moment," says Edward.

"You're the best tree I've ever known but please leave me alone."

"One Eye, go outside and keep a lookout, I need to tell Jon what you told me," says Edward. One Eye nods and goes outside. Edward yells at Jon but he doesn't hear it, all he hears are the waves crashing on some distant, storm-torn shore.

Edward finally pulls Jon to his feet and they stumble out into the corridor with One Eye leading the way. Edward's only hope is that some of what he said got through to Jon. He didn't seem to be there anymore. His eyes were vacant the whole time Edward was speaking. This is what Edward is thinking as they turn the corner, into a firing squad.

Everything slows down. It's an ambush and before One Eye can react, the shots ring out. Several hit One Eye square in the chest, exploding into his flesh. Life and death are sometimes simple. This is one of those times. Death is simple here. One Eye falls and the blood from his wounds comes out in splashes of red against the air around him. He dies as he falls. Things fall. He is one of them. The hole in his chest does not hurt him for more than a moment but it rips the souls out of Edward and Jon. His eye stays open as his head hits the ground, last.

Edward roars and dives at them. Bullets scream into his wooden skin but he keeps moving and green sap fills the air as his splintered body falls into them like a deadly, thrashing thorn bush, impaling throats and hearts and minds. Human and ent scream, in mortal terror, in inhuman anger.

Everyone is dead, so suddenly, so imperfectly, so simply.

Everything is going to be ok.

Jon steps over the bodies and through his tears, he unwraps the cloth around One Eye's head. Slowly, a young man with red hair and pale skin is revealed. He has an angelic face with one bright green eye that now, will always look at forever. A photograph of a young woman holding One Eye as he sleeps on a couch falls from the black wrappings. In the foreground of the picture, a child that shares both their features plays in front of a television.

Jon falls to his knees. He holds Edward's and One Eye's hands and he screams trying to hold as much of both of them as he can, throwing himself into their bodies, screaming into them, screaming into the end of their lives. More guards come. A gun slams into the back of his head. They pick him up and drag him to the doctor's laboratory. He does not resist.

CHAPTER 34

NOW

Nothing.

Jon is strapped into the machine but they leave his arms alone, as he's not struggling. He remembers a bird with broken wings: "Leave it for the cats," his mother had said and he hadn't, he'd tried to save it but it died three days later and he didn't know what to do with the body so he just held it and cried until his mother found him in his room and she was angry.

A nurse loads a flash drive into the side of the machine and pictures and symbols flash across the screen in front of him. The first symbol is a man on a cross. The second is a trench filled with what look like hundreds of skinny, dead bodies. Then a burnt landscape with nothing but ash in the air. A child being stalked by a vulture. Then the news report of Elliot Philips, the astronaut that got spun out into space, then a picture of a soldier dying and playing guitar on a battlefield. Then a single piece of paper with the most beautiful sentence in the world written on it. Then the diary of an abused woman. Then a screenshot of gamers' chats. And on. And on. And on.

You have read this all before.

"I'm going to need drugs for this."

A man with a thin black mustache yells at a crowd, who salute at a forty-five degree angle. The woman places several guitars, a noose, various trinkets, and a single nail in various compartments around the machine.

"You'll get them. All you want and more."

Bombs fall from a plane into little pockets of fire on the ground.

A man in a white lab coat walks in, pushing a tray piled high with vials of Sadness. One hundred white people surround a black man hanging by his neck.

"Jesus."

Children stand around, covered in coal dust, poor as the dirt, staring at the camera.

"This may destroy your brain if you live through this but I imagine there's not much left anyway."

A plane slams into the side of a building. And again.

"My mind might be a little off these days but my heart is still here, which is more than I can say for you."

A building collapses.

The doctor snorts.

"Your emotions have made you stupid."

A monk sets himself on fire.

"Just fucking kill me."

But the doctor carries on, "Do you remember a young boy called Wilfred? A child you helped escape from your school, on the day of The End? Do you remember turning into a shadow and killing him? Do you remember killing your mother, Jon? What did you tell yourself? That she'd left? That she'd killed herself?"

Jon turns away and shuts his eyes.

There is a casual acceptance within him. This will kill him. This will kill him but at least the world will be better for his death. It'll be under the control of the doctor and whomever else he represented but at least it'll live. It'll be able to be ok. He prepares to die.

They continue to load symbols and books and objects into the machine and now, they start to pour vial after vial of Sadness into the IV attached to Jon's arm. Then, they turn the machine on.

It hits him with the force of a thousand lovers turning away in bed. It hits him with a thousand late nights spent away from home. It hits him with the death of a thousand mothers and fathers.

He gasps with sadness and something begins to burn inside him.

His mind is a black ocean rolling over itself and his tiny bark is nothingness itself and all he has to hold onto.

As the waves boil higher and higher and he feels himself slipping into insanity, he has a vision of himself and Edward back in his cell and Edward is trying to tell him something, grabbing his hand and shaking it, trying to bring his attention to it, trying to get through the dark water to remind him of what they'd intended if this happened. They'd known that there would be Sadness involved in the process somehow but not this much. Jon needs one single moment of clarity for this to work. He doesn't get it.

Kurt Cobain's guitar. The tattoo of a dead father's wife.

He uses every fibre of his shaking body to roll over and bring his hand up to his mouth, making it look like he's clenching down on it out of pain but really, he's squeezing a vial of normal, everyday tap water into his mouth. Tap water that contains the happiness drugs the United Government pours in by the barrel. He can't control his chattering teeth and he bites down on the glass and shatters it in his mouth; the liquid runs down his throat and he does his best to spit out the leftover glass.

The doctor's eyes go wide when he sees the blood pouring out of his mouth.

"He's biting off his tongue! Stop him! He needs to live a little bit longer for this to work!"

Jon, through the blood, smiles as dark sparks start to shoot in front of his eyes. A guard starts to scream and clutch his head.

CHAPTER 35

NOW

Everything.

The guards have no control over themselves anymore. They're surrounded by their worst, most hellish fears and they kill each other, mercilessly, with whatever's at hand. One drives a beaker through his friend's chest, killing the monster that's always lived under his bed; another beats on someone else's face, seeing only the man who molested him when he was a child; another strangles himself, trying to stop his very essence from escaping his throat. They see what Jon wants them to see and Jon is holding nothing back. The drugs coursing through his veins propel his mind to terrible depths and he slays them with pure fear and horror as he steps out of the chair, no one even tries to stop him.

His father nearly destroyed the world.

He will finish the job.

The Sadness and the artifacts of sadness were all given to him to ensure he finished the job. The happiness drugs in the tap water that Edward gave him let him break free, let him rise up to kill them all, to take the world with him. Black flames lick his body as he staggers forward and the doctor backs away and then runs out the door, out to the spires outside of the United Government building, to get away from the burning madman. Jon, or whatever he's become, follows him. The doctor hides behind one of the small walls by the steps going up the spire, next to one of the guards.

"Why is it always light? Why whenever anything crazy happens with this guy, it's always preceded by light?" The doctor doesn't even turn to look at the young guard but he talks anyway.

"Because whatever he and his father are or were, it comes from the things we once worshiped. First, from the sun. Then, from fire. And when it was more widely available, electricity."

"But why does he have a dark light?"

"Because there is nothing left to worship," the doctor shoves the guard out, into Jon's path and he's immediately consumed by the dark fire, spreading from Jon in waves. He screams and falls from the edge of the stairs, down a thousand floors and his body hits one of the old teleportation safety nets below, killing him instantly and causing the old technology to flicker slightly. It draws the attention of the people below. The distraction doesn't buy the doctor much time but he takes the time he has and runs further up, up, always up. Jon climbs the steps and the light starts to grow strange inside Jon's head and odd contrasts dance slowly in his periphery. No one should be able swallow this much Sadness and survive. He doesn't expect to. The steps become a water-fall, then molten lava, then everything stupid he's ever said. He tries to force himself not to think about the steps, or how far away the doctor is, or how long he has before he becomes an emotional thermonuclear explosion, before he ends the world just like his father before him.

Just the step in front. It's over after each step is done and it starts again with the next, one hundred battles to the roof. Someone has sold him fake firewood. He's upset. He laughs. Things stop making sense as the world turns faster and the compass in his head ticks slowly on. Somewhere the world is turning again. He drives backwards in time, hoping to reach himself as a teenager, to go back to that night when he first met Michelle and they smoked cigarettes in the park, to the last few hours before he discovered all this, before the world ended, before everything changed. Instead, he finds the doctor, backed up against the edge of the walkway at the top of the spire. Jon stumbles and the flames flicker. The doctor smiles. Jon leans down and picks up a half-smoked cigarette and puts it in his mouth. He holds his finger underneath it and the black flames ignite an ember on the end. He exhales the smoke and coughs, then looks at the doctor through pitch black eyes. "It's time for a change, Doctor."

"I'm not a fighting man," says the doctor. "But for you, I will make an exception." He lashes out suddenly with a small Charge Stick™ he's kept hidden in his lab coat and he strikes Jon through the face. The cigarette goes tumbling and waves of brutal current course through Jon's head, scrambling the last of his thoughts. Jon falls to his knees.

There is nothing left of him.

He looks up through a mess of blood and tears. And he smiles. He reaches inside his pocket and takes out the folded, bloody picture he took off One Eye's body. There's One Eye, sleeping on the lap of the woman he loves and his child, playing on the floor in front of them. He looks at it and slowly lets it seep into his mind and replace the thousands of images the doctor's machine infested his brain with. They flicker off like snow falling into shadows, like a film reel slowing down and for one brief moment, he knows what real love looks and feels like.

It is enough.

He slowly focuses all his energy on the doctor's brain. The doctor can feel Jon getting inside.

"No," he says, realising what Jon's about to do. But it's too late. He's inside the doctor's head. He's in my head. You are in my head. Jon gives him pain. I give him pain. I take the pain Edward and One Eye gave me in their dying moments and send it towards the doctor in a blinding ball of hurt. It sends him flying, clutching his head. Jon goes flying, experiencing what he wants the doctor to experience, hurting himself as much as he wants to hurt the doctor, making him feel what he feels.

Jon throws himself over the edge of the spire.

The doctor throws himself over the edge of the spire.

They fall over the edge of the spire.

He fell. I fell. We fell.

I imagine the first time I felt pain. I cut my foot on a broken bottle in my parents' driveway. My head explodes. Jon's head explodes. A wave of black light echoes outwards from what's left of Jon's soul. Suddenly, everyone left in the last city on Earth looks up and everyone across the planet, the survivors, even the man in Africa, feels the same thing and they remember the first time they hurt themselves as a child; some fall off bikes, some graze their knees, some nearly die.

Jon falls.

He remembers, with every fibre of his being, what it felt like when his mother wrapped a bandage around his foot. And everyone below remembers what it felt like to be helped.

Some are kissed better, some are picked up off the floor, some are given a meal.

He remembers not being able to let Michelle in the house when he was a teenager, he remembers what it felt like to have love denied and so does everyone else, hands waving at a station platform, the burst of light that swallowed them whole, or the cancer that took them slowly.

And he falls.

And he sends out his consciousness as a story, in a book, and he infects pages with his story. He believes it and he makes it real and his mind eats up stories and pixels and ink and the writing changes, page, after page, after page.

Now you know the truth about me. You are holding the last of me. Your eyes reading these words are the only things that keep me existing. When you stop reading, Jon stops existing. I stop existing. You make me real. You make me real. You make me real.

Please make me real.

I make up a day on a beach somewhere. Jon makes up a day on a beach somewhere; he forces himself to imagine how white the sand is, each and every individual grain, he starts to feel them under his feet, then the water, just the right shade of blue, crystal clear, a fisherman in the background, the sun going down, a quiet electricity in the air. A whole day, a day that lasts forever, a beach where time and place don't matter and everyone feels it. Everyone feels it.

Here, in this place, Emily walks across the white sand, in front of the burning sun and Jon puts his hands on her hips and they kiss for the first and last and only time and it lasts forever. They have children and grow old and his beard goes grey and they die and they come back as babies and they love each other the very first time they see each other, and it happens a million, million times, in some other world, where all this is just a story which keeps him and Emily alive, each time the story is read.

All this is just a story. We are so real somewhere else.

He stops falling and the last thought to go through his mind is that it feels like somewhere, someone is touching the same road as him, at the same time.

And Jon knows what it feels like to feel nothing at all.

In the distance, a man thinks he sees someone falling from the spire.

But it could be just crows and shadows.

EPILOGUE

Emily wasn't in the building when the United Government raided Duer. She was out.

Sometimes, life and death are simple like that.

With a renewed sense of purpose and a direction, the last people on Earth left the city of NewLand and spread out across the countryside. Because there was no one left in the city, there was nothing left to govern and no need for a government.

They left in small groups because humans are social creatures and they enjoy the company of others, especially if they're no longer being fed antidepressants on a daily basis and are, in fact, naturally happy or naturally anything for that matter. They went north, east, south, and west. Some by bike, some by boat, some on foot.

Slowly, humanity starts again.

Michelle, the real one, marries someone who makes her happy.

Right now, Emily is cycling west down a highway, towards a setting sun and amongst the things she has deemed worth keeping, all strapped to the bicycle or pulled behind in the makeshift trailer. In that trailer is a potted plant containing a fragile, young sapling that though damaged and burnt, looks like it might still live. She calls it Edward.

She grows older. Everyone grows older.

I do not know if this happens.

But it is what I like to think happens, as I fall.

THE END

You have read this all before and you will again. Do you think you're in the bookshop now, just browsing? Are you in front of your computer, previewing the first few pages? Or is this a well-thumbed tattered old thing that lives next to your bed? Or is it sleeping, lost and forgotten at the back of a bookshelf?

No matter. You have read this all before and you will again.

Have you ever stopped and wondered if, really, you're just living the same few seconds over and over again and you just don't know it? You'd never know. Maybe you've been doing the same thing for one thousand years. Sometimes that happens. Like when you're reading and you get a thought stuck in your head and you find your eyes just glazing over the words and you have to go back and read the same thing again.

No matter. You have read this all before and you will again.

You have read this before.

This is what happens, when I fall.

CHAPTER 1

NOW

Something incredibly sad.

What follows is what happens each time I fall. I do not know if these things really happen but this is what I believe happens. As your eyes move across these words, some sacred engine is coming back to life and I am beginning to fall again. Sometimes, it feels like floating.

If you do not mind, I will refer to myself as Jon, in the third person, as these things happen.

I understand that talking about Jon as "I" instead of "Jon" would perhaps make more sense, as I am the one telling you what's happening, not some omniscient voice somewhere up in the clouds. But one of my earliest memories is of my father, narrating the things I did as I ran around the house or played outside. Like a commentator for a football match, he would yell, "Jon goes up the swing and down the swing, look at him go! He's a champion!" or "Jon's eating his spaghetti like a master, ladies and gentlemen, let's see if he can finish in time or if we'll have another disaster like we did with the vegetables the other night!"

So talking about himself in the third person in his mind, where no one but you gets to go, gives Jon (still me) a certain degree of confidence. Or maybe it's just that old habits die hard. Anyway, this is now and in this now, this is what's happening to the remaining humans in the last city on Earth.

"A space station has recovered Eliot Philips, an astronaut who was spun out into space in a refueling

accident and now, his body has returned after completing an orbit around the earth which has lasted
more than thirty years."

The screen on the side of the giant black floating news zeppelin shows a picture of an old woman, presumably Philips' widow, identifying a young frozen corpse as she weeps tears she has been holding on to for far too long. The zeppelin hovers like a bumblebee over the city. Below the floating news screen, the white marble spires of the United Government building, the last great monument man has built, reach for the heavens, each one raised as if in a challenge to some unseen and unknown adversary. Jon turns to look at them, breaking the audio feed into his head from the news zeppelin and the sudden silence brings to an end his wandering day dream. He can make out the building's spires all the way on the other side of NewLand, past the mostly empty and unused ornate buildings, lecture rooms, theaters and gymnasiums that blossom strictly from each side of the intricate streets, even through the grimy windows of Emily's hodgepodge, trinket-filled apartment. Low-hanging old lights cast a strange glow over the room and are complemented by the flickering lights from one of the first teleporters ever made. The teleporter hums for a second, like it might spring back to life, but it doesn't. It's broken forever. The government has asked that Emily collect and keep old things, should the world ever need them again. Marble statues from Greece, stone slabs containing fossils from Africa and a rainbow coloured VW Beetle from the American 60's all live uneasily together. The government likes giving people responsibilities. Jon thinks that they believe it gives people a sense of purpose.

NewLand feels like an old attic, spilling over with old secrets. Like someone has taken the leftovers of the world and dumped them in one place. This place. The last living place. Through the window, Jon regards one impossibly perverse spire which has bits of the Eiffel Tower sticking out of it. It was rudely salvaged, and carelessly erected. Industrial teleporters—when they were still allowed—brought it here along with the Acropolis, the Statue of Liberty, and several other things that were considered "worth keeping." It acts as a reminder of what the human race was once capable. Now there are less than a few million people left on the planet. Black smoke rises out of stacks from the dark machines rumbling below the building, the only noise to be heard as figures move silently from building to building. The grey buildings are all closely piled together like set pieces in a play, short balconies hanging over doors, just a few steps from their neighbour across the road. Some people have painted their doors bright, festive colours but most are a simple, uniform grey. It is a terminally depressed world and yet the people drift past, each individual wearing an immovable grin. No, that's wrong. Some grinned. Some smiled. Some raised their eyebrows and smiled with their eyes, and no one said much. What's left to talk about? How happy you are? People live, die, and smile as they do each.

It's been nearly ten years since the world ended. Or it may as well have. Jon's a man in the twilight of his twenties now and his delicate frame holds his clothes as best it can.

Outside, across the road from him, a little blonde girl in a pink dress runs down the pavement outside into her father's sweat-soaked arms. The father shoots wildly with a stolen pistol at the police teleporting in, who are yelling at him to stop. As she grips his neck with her tiny arms and holds tight, a single shot fired from a young sergeant hits the father in the shoulder, sending a spray of blood into the air, just missing his daughter's head. His blue eyes go red and his face grimaces in pain, but still he instinctively whips his body in front of her, his only daughter, and they fall backwards into the bright blue light behind them; a light coming from the stolen government teleporter the man, apparently, has illegally modified. And then silence for a second. Then a little blonde girl in a pink dress suddenly appears outside and runs down the pavement outside into her father's arms, who's shot in the shoulder, again. They have looped like this, for years. They're just ghosts. The theory is that the man's illegal modifications caused this infinite loop but no one really seems to know what causes the teleporters to loop, just that they do. And now humankind must deal with chronological waste sites, where teleporters have terminally jammed. It must watch the same thing, again and again.

There are thousands of these waste sites and these ghosts are the reason that access to technology has been extremely limited. Jon stops watching. He's been absent-mindedly playing with his father's brass pocket watch, turning it over and over in his hands, feeling the engraving with his fingers: *You will become whatever you want to become.* He returns it to his inside jacket pocket, where it's close to his heart. The view of this particular ghost, this endless loop of a quite famous bank robber trying to rescue or kidnap his daughter—depending on who you speak to or what newspaper you read; there are only two newspapers that are still published for the remaining populace, and they still disagree with each other—once drove the property prices sky-high amongst the last humans.

But now, this place, like the little girl outside, is just another ghost.

If teleportation were still allowed, at least the food from the one remaining commercial airline wouldn't be wasted. It could simply be teleported off the plane, onto the table of any starving person. There were once plenty of starving people, all over the world. But not now. Back then, everyone wanted to work in New York, have lunch in Paris and pay rent in rural India. But no one figured on the ghosts. People got caught in endless loops when the machines malfunctioned or were modified or were used on Sundays. The excuses were numerous but it soon became clear that the technology just wasn't stable. At first, the looping ghosts were shrouded with tarpaulins, wherever and however it was happening, surrounded by police tape but people seemed to care less and less and many found some kind of fascination in watching moments and people repeat themselves endlessly. The people in them never know. For them, it is always now.

Jon is full of these things, feelings and thoughts, not just in his heart but in his head. The first thing taken out in the war that followed The End, the common name for the day it all went to shit, the great reckoning of mankind, was the Statue of Liberty. If you squint you can see the remaining bits: a spike from her crown, an eyebrow, a hand with a torch. Apparently, you can still see the book she once held, if you get close enough. Bombers dropped a billion tons of hate and fire on it. Jon should know, he used to fly one of those bombers. They were told that they were destroying an enemy but he can't remember the details. No one was allowed to remember the details. Now, even without the memories and with so few things left, the war was clearly about resources. The remains of the earth. Mankind has been reduced to a scavenging dog and its ribs are showing. Besides the algae farms far outside of NewLand, there's barely a patch of land left on the planet that can grow even the stubbornest weed.

He turns his head and looks past the remains of the Eiffel Tower, to get a better look at Lady Liberty's crown of thorns. This is another thing he keeps inside himself, this piece of knowledge about the bombings, the things that cause ruins and remains and survivors. It is a thing that makes him clench his jaw. He knows they take the families of "enemy" aviators and strap them, alive, to the sides of their aircraft in glass coffins. Military airfields are often filled with screams before takeoff, as young girls and boys, wives, mothers and fathers are lead towards the aircraft to be strapped in. And so all pilots know that when they shoot at the enemy, there's a chance that they're killing their own, or a friend's family.

And while the pilots weep as they fight, neither side's generals allow themselves to care. This is/was/could be war, after all. Thousands lived. More died. There doesn't seem to be much enemy left. Or anyone really.

Jon carries on looking out the dirty window and stretches his long fingers out and back in again and again like he's squeezing an invisible ball. His fingers miss playing with the pocket watch but that habit irritates him. Faint memories of what once happened crash through his mind. Different memories do the same in the street, through the weak, tenuous fabric of now, riddled with holes from billions of people jumping back and forth from place to place, shadows and glimmers, caught in loops forever.

Jon tells his head to shut up and he picks up a tiny rust-red vial off the Venetian-carved antique table. He examines the lime-green writing on it before holding it above his mouth. He can't read the word properly but he thinks it starts with an "S." Exactly three drops land on his tongue and he counts them off carefully as they fall.

Lacrymatory: Lat. lacrima - a tear. A bottle used to collect the tears of mourners at funerals, found in ancient Roman and Greek tombs, normally made of glass but occasionally also terra cotta.

The drops taste like peach iced tea. It is sweet, not harsh at all.

"What's this one called?" asks Jon, swallowing, turning the vial over and over in his hands.

"Saudade," says Emily, "It's a Portuguese word for the almost terminal, endless longing for a lost love."

"Cute."

She can hear him because she's spent a good portion of her life practicing hearing him, no matter how quietly he speaks. Her red hair follows her shoulders down her back and her eyes are deep blue, deeper than Jon's, speckled with flint and green. Jon does not think about the curves behind her Victorian blue dress. They are friends and always have been, nothing more. Jon, instead, thinks that Saudade, the drug he's just put on his tongue which causes one to be overwhelmed by emotion, is a bit like Limerence (again, another word used to describe an endless longing for love) or Stendhal Syndrome (the term used to describe being bought to tears by a work of art), which is what he'd had the first time he'd tried Sadness with her. But this has slightly more of a body rush because he can feel the tips of his fingers start to tingle and go numb. He walks around Emily's dirty, cluttered little apartment, which is filled with antiques and the bric-a-brac of mankind, while his legs can still hold him, hands still opening and closing, breathing like they're lungs. His eyes glance out the window, sick of the bank robber and his daughter with the blonde hair and the pink dress looping outside, hoping in vain for something more moving to look at. *Please, God, give me something else to look at than an old fire escape and this hopeful, desperate father.* Still, the fire escape with its rust and its textures has its own kind of nobility, a defiance of some kind, because it still stands, which is so much more than can be said of so many things these days.

In the distance, he thinks he sees someone falling from the top spire of the United Government building. But it might just be crows and shadows.